The Misfits Save the World

An Aran Islands Fantasy

Therese Gilardi

The Misfits Save The World

By Therese Gilardi

ISBN: 978-0-9862811-9-8

Cover Art Designed by LJP Book Design

For all the misfits

ONE

All across Dublin letters went out to the misfits. Invitations, which were really thinly veiled commands, directing the 14-year-olds to report to St. Dymphna's Holiday Academy by the end of the week. Parents, heads of school and members of the public at large had nominated them for attendance, with the hope they would abandon their wayward paths. Before it was too late.

Freya O'Callahan had been reading a book of mathematical formulas when she heard the letter slide through the post slot in the battered front door of the shabby flat she shared with her mother and younger sisters. She carefully set the book up high, out of Nora and Allie's reach (she hated the thought of the twins' sticky fingers marring the library book) and hurried to the front hall. A long envelope the color of caramel trifle lay on the warped wooden floor. It was addressed to Freya O'Callahan and Legal Guardian. She slid her fingernail across the seal and pulled out a thin stack of papers. The top page was stamped with an official looking seal.

Freya O'Callahan is directed to report
to St. Dymphna's Holiday Academy
Inis Mor

Freya clutched the letter to her chest. She had never heard of St. Dymphna's Holiday Academy, but the name sounded magical. Freya had seen adverts for summer camps. Ireland was full of different programs, some dedicated to special focuses or hobbies. Freya longed to attend one for maths. She could see herself at a lodge in the forest, or maybe by a beach, where she would be able to work on algebra and word problems and perhaps even study physics, since it was kind of related. The type of place where everyone got their own calculator, instead of having to borrow one from school, and she could fill as many a5 notebooks as she wanted. There would be time to lie in the slivers of sun that sliced across Ireland in summer and melt chocolate bars over a fire pit. Best of all, Freya would be free from having to tend to the twins. And she wouldn't have to nip out to the off-license to fetch Mam a fresh bottle of whiskey, or call her father, begging him to come back, even though everyone knew he would never return.

Her mother had been wrong. Clearly the nuns at Holy Ghost didn't hate her, since they must have been the ones who had recommended Freya for such an honor. Finally, things were turning her way. Freya pulled out her phone. She wanted to see the photos of the camp, maybe there were even reviews. Would she need camping gear? Snacks? Freya's fingers shook as she inserted St. Dymphna's Holiday Academy into the search bar.

"No! There must be some mistake."

Freya hit the refresh button. Cleared her search history. Started again.

But there had been no mistake.

St. Dymphna's was not a holiday camp for gifted and talented students.

St. Dymphna's was a school for incorrigibles.

On the other side of the Liffey, Quinn McMalley was lying on the velvet settee his mother had brought back from Paris on her latest antique buying trip. Glynnis ran one of the most famous vintage furniture and clothing emporiums in Ireland. People came over from all parts of the capitol, even from the Continent, to see the way she displayed her wares. Glynnis, Oliver and their five children were all impeccable in every way. Except for Quinn, who was remarkable for his ordinariness in a family of over-achievers. The only thing outstanding about Quinn was his looks. He resembled a Roman god come to life, with his strong chin, golden hair, green eyes and aptitude for archery.

"Darling, must you put your trainers on the furniture?" Glynnis frowned at her son.

She'd often wondered how her youngest son had turned out so different than the others, whose bulletin boards and walls were crowded with ribbons and awards. Perhaps it was her fault. She'd been so smitten when she'd first seen Quinn, so charmed as the years went on with his winning smile and his interest in bees. Maybe that was where it had all gone wrong, at the greenhouse on her parents' estate, where she'd let Quinn tend to the hives when he should have been working on his sums or reading something other than nature magazines.

It was Oliver who first heard about St. Dymphna's Holiday Academy. He'd a colleague whose nephew was facing the abyss where his future was concerned. Once Glynnis had realized the similarities between that boy and Quinn, she'd become afraid. Visions of Quinn never leaving the house, never obtaining a degree let alone a job, began to keep her up at night until she could stand it no more. She'd written to the director of St. Dymphna's.

The letter from the Holiday Academy felt heavy in her hand. She toyed with the envelope for a moment, considering whether she should abandon the idea altogether. But Oliver's patience with Quinn was now as thin as a reed, and some of their friends were starting to talk. Not to her face, of course, but she'd seen them, changing the subject quickly whenever they spoke of their own children's accomplishments. The day was fast approaching when Quinn would prove to be a liability. An embarrassment, and Glynnis would not tolerate that. No, there was no other option.

She stepped into the conservatory, her voice high. "I've a surprise for you."

Quinn didn't look away from the notebook perched in his lap. Another drawing of a beehive, heaven help him. Glynnis straightened her already rod-like back and strode over to her son.

"This came for you."

"What is it?"

"Read it, please."

"Why don't you?"

Glynnis frowned. Must she do everything for the boy?

"It's an ... invitation. No, a summons. You're to report to St. Dymphna's Holiday Academy on Tuesday."

"Whatever that is, I'm not interested."

"You don't have a choice."

Quinn looked up at his mother. Glynnis never said he didn't have a choice. He stretched out his hand for the letter, then scanned the contents.

"What," he asked, "Is this place?"

Freya's mother was already down for the day, even though it was barely half one. She was lying across her unmade bed, face down, arms wide. Freya sighed. It was so unfair, having to be the mother when she was only fifteen.

"Get up," Freya demanded from the door.

She walked across the creaky floor boards and hovered over her mother. The smell of stale whiskey and cigarettes grew stronger the closer Freya leaned toward the bed. Freya didn't expect her mother to acknowledge her presence. She rarely did, unless she needed something. To her surprise, Freya's mother rolled onto her side and propped herself up on her left elbow.

"You got the letter."

"You knew?"

Freya's mother shrugged. "I'd heard rumors."

She glanced over at the dresser, littered with old tissues, collapsed plastic drinking cups and two empty bottles.

"What is this place, and why are you sending me there?"

"It's a camp for ... self-improvement."

"The only one who needs improving 'round here is you."

"Watch your language young lady, you're my daughter. Show some respect."

"You don't deserve my respect. Or anyone else's. No wonder Da left."

It happened so fast Freya was caught unaware. One moment her mother was perched in her usual spot atop the pillows, then the next instant her hand was across Freya's cheek. Freya felt her skin smart. Her flesh stung from the slap.

"That's why you're going to this program. You don't care for anyone but yourself. You've left all of us no choice."

Freya was still rubbing her cheek. "At least I'll have a break from you."

She ran to the bedroom she shared with the twins and climbed into the top bunk. Although Freya acted brave in front of her mother, she was scared. She'd never been outside of County Dublin, not even on the holidays they'd taken when her father was still part of the family. She wasn't ever allowed to leave her rough little corner of the city. Far too often she felt like a dog whose lead was too tight, but at least she knew where to find shelter if she was being harassed. Or, as happened last week when she was returning home with a pack of cigarettes and a bottle of whiskey for her mother, robbed by a group looking for trouble.

Freya wondered about Inis Mor and the west. She'd heard they spoke Irish and that there were no proper cities, not even real roads. Visions of the horror stories she'd read about reform schools, with teachers quick with a ruler and poor food rations, made her squirm. Two months in the rural backlands. Maybe Freya had been wrong.

Maybe her life could get worse.

TWO

The days leading up to the departure for St. Dymphna's were the longest of Quinn's life. His brothers and sisters had already left for the summer holidays. They were off digging wells in arid lands, ladling out food to the hungry in developing countries and engaging in all manner of good works. Oddly enough, they never asked Quinn to accompany them. Which was fine, as summer on the estate on the edge of Dublin was his favorite season. He looked forward to the endless hours with his beloved bees. His grandfather had given him a handful of hives last year. They were tucked away in the greenhouse, beyond the family conservatory, on a private spit of land no one else ever visited. It was Quinn's favorite part of the property.

For the first time, Quinn's parents refused to back down. He'd been so certain he would be able to talk them out of sending him away. He'd even forced himself to cry as he begged not to attend the holiday academy, peering out between his fingers so he could study their reactions as fat tears rolled down his cheeks. To Quinn's shock, Oliver and Glynnis weren't particularly moved by his histrionics. Which was quite a shame as it was one of his better performances. They'd merely waited until he finished sobbing, then retired to their room for the night.

Glynnis especially seemed to have grown a hard shell full of daggers over her heart. She had taken to having the housekeeper wake Quinn for an early breakfast. She claimed it was high time he got used to keeping to a schedule. Even worse, she'd begun insisting Quinn carry his cleats and football to the closet, instead of just leaving them lying about the house.

"Funny story, Oliver," Quinn had said one night at dinner after his father told them about a barrister who had tripped twice during his courtroom entrance that morning.

"You have to stop addressing us by our proper names," Oliver replied. "You're too old for that nonsense."

Quinn's back stiffened. Up until now, his parents had seemed charmed, or at least tolerated it, when Quinn called them Glynnis and Oliver. Quinn was both enraged and embarrassed.

When the departure day arrived, his father was arguing a case in court and his mother had a new shipment of armoires arriving from France, so they passed Quinn off to their driver. He was rather hurt. Although he'd never admit it, it seemed like no one would even miss him. Except his bees. He'd trekked to the greenhouse one last time to check on the hives, and forced the gardener to pledge he'd keep tabs on them until Quinn returned. Still, he was worried. What if Rodman forgot? He couldn't bear the thought of coming home to a dead colony.

"No worries, your wee winged creatures will be grand," Agnes, the family chauffeur, assured Quinn as she drove toward the bus depot.

St. Dymphna's had chartered a bus to ferry the summer "guests" as they were called to County Galway. Quinn had been on airport shuttles and luxury coaches the football coach ordered for the team when they had a match out of town, but he'd never been on anything like the long buses housed in the Bus Eireann depot on the north side of the city.

Agnes glided into a spot near the depot, grabbed Quinn's gear from the boot and gave him an awkward pat on the shoulder before turning him loose. Quinn strapped his bags over his shoulder, took a deep breath and strode inside. At the far end of the terminal, a group of kids around his age stood in an awkward half circle. The group was about half boys, half girls, all getting disdainful looks from the other travelers in the bus depot. Quinn groaned. From what he could tell, not one of them looked like anyone he'd ever want to call friend.

Freya had taken the city bus to the bus depot. She struggled a bit with her bags, although the inconvenience was more than outweighed by the joy of traveling on her own. Finally, Freya would have an adventure. She'd borrowed a few euros from her mother's bureau on the way out so she could buy a chocolate bar for breakfast. As she waited in line to pay at the snack bar, two women strode in from the departures hall and cut in front of her.

"Excuse me, I'm next at the till."

They looked past her, as if she was not there. Freya sighed. She was so sick of being invisible. When it was her turn, she plonked the money on the counter and headed back to the comfort of the plastic chairs in the departures hall. Slowly other people her age began to stagger into the bus depot, carrying enough gear to last a summer. Outside the station, the kind of long car Freya imagined people rode in if they lived in posh detached houses with private gardens and central heat that worked stopped at the curb. A driver with a cap hopped out of the car and opened the door. A tall boy, so perfect he looked like he'd been airbrushed, stumbled out of the car. The driver fetched his bags from the boot and gave him an awkward half hug before zooming out into the traffic.

The boy looked around for a moment, then walked toward the band of kids who had gathered near a sign reading "St. Dymphna's Holiday Academy." Freya smiled. Clearly St. Dymphna's wasn't as bad as she feared. A rich kid with a chauffeur and matching bags wouldn't be going to a rugged reform school for losers. Her first instinct had been right. This would be a fun vacation. She would have the summer to herself. Long stretches of time to be alone with her thoughts. No one would climb on her lap or scream while she was trying to read.

A guy with a hideous green shirt and jeans that managed to be too tight even though he was so slender you could barely see him when he turned sideways stood in front of the St. Dymphna's sign. He looked around the waiting area before blowing a whistle so shrill Freya was sure he'd deafened dogs for miles around.

"Attention those of youse here for the trip to St. Dymphna's. We'll be lining up for boarding in ten minutes. Say your good-byes now."

Freya edged forward and looked around the lounge. A boy she was certain worked at The Right Rice curry take-away near the park stood with his family. A small girl in a glittery dress hung off of his right arm. He didn't seem bothered at all, which Freya could not imagine. She hated the way the twins were constantly touching her body. A man, who must be the boy's father, they looked like carbon copies of each other, scowled as he read the departures board. A pretty woman in a bright pink and red sari stood next to the little sister. She glanced over at her husband. When she saw he was looking away, she pulled a bag of sweets from her bag. Freya recognized the brand. It was quite dear. Her mouth watered at the memory. She'd eaten them on holiday when her da still lived at home. Even then, Mam had been rather stingy in doling them out from their shiny wrappers. Freya watched as the mother looked over at the father once more. He was peering over his glasses, his back now firmly to the family. The mother unzipped the boy's bag, dropped in the sweets and quickly closed the sack. Freya scanned the rest of the kids waiting to board the St. Dymphna's coach.

"Please say something," a low voice begged.

Freya turned around, trying not to be too obvious. Another boy, this one with big green eyes and hair the color and consistency of twigs after they've been blown from a tree during a windstorm, was staring around the room. He didn't seem to focus on anything, nor to hear his mother.

"Tadgh."

Still he didn't reply.

Tadgh had the largest contingency with him, the makings of a true send-off party. There were at least ten people, all focused on the boy in the long sleeved dark blue t-shirt so stiff it must have stood in a pressing cupboard all night. He ignored them all, instead twisting the tag attached to his bag over and over. Freya frowned. If she had that many people interested in her, blowing them off would be the last thing on her mind.

The linoleum floor echoed from the click-clack of someone tapping her way toward the boarding area. A girl with so much dark red curly hair piled on top of her head Freya thought at first she was wearing one of the wigs people wear to step dance was coming toward her. The girl seemed to glide across the floor, moving to a song only she could hear, her feet stomping out a beat as her brother? boyfriend? carried her battered bag, which was covered in dance decals. He laid the bag down, nodded at the girl and left. Clearly he was a brother, not a boyfriend.

A number of other kids and their families rushed past, clogging the lounge until the skinny guy blew his whistle. People fell in line, bags hanging from their arms, as a girl and another guy, also in the same hideous green shirts and wearing whistles around their necks, smiled at the assembled family and friends.

"No worries, we'll take care of your loved ones. They'll be grand, you have our word," the girl said.

"You won't recognize them upon their return," the guy added.

"Here's hoping," someone called out.

"We'll hold you to that," a man yelled.

There was a round of awkward laughter.

Freya's back stiffened. That didn't sound very promising. She liked herself, in spite of the terrible things her mother always said. She'd zero interest in returning as someone new.

"Right then, on you go."

Freya followed the group. To her surprise, they walked toward a luxury coach. Her spirits soared. This was the way to start a vacation. But then the skinny guy strode past the luxurious coaches parked in the bay, to a ratty bus lodged behind the others. She could taste the petrol in the air as the bus wheezed. She looked up at at the driver. He didn't look like he was in much better shape. Freya glanced around. No one else seemed alarmed. It was just, she told herself, her lack of familiarity with travel making her nervous. When it was her turn, she climbed the steep steps.

A number of kids had already boarded. Freya had never seen so many teenagers interested in bunching together in the seats up front, near the driver. Not only that, but everyone was quiet, looking at and nodding toward the minders in the hideous green t-shirts. Freya rolled her eyes.

The five seats across the back row, extra wide and up a step, appeared to be empty. Freya strode down the aisle and took her place on the middle cushion. It was only after she sat that she noticed the silent boy, bent in half, checking something on the ground in front of his seat next to the window.

"Hey," she said.

He stared up at Freya. He didn't reply. She wasn't scared of him, the way she had been afraid of the creepy old man who leaned against the counter at the off-license and watched as she begged for yet another bottle on credit. Rather, Freya was fascinated by this kid, who watched her intently. A moment later, when the boy with the packet of sweets tucked into his bag took the seat between them, he stared at him as well.

"Turkish delight?" The guy with the sweets asked.

He had a low voice, glasses that sat on the edge of his nose and a slight dimple on his right cheek.

"No, thanks," Freya replied. The chocolate bar, a rare treat, had been a huge mistake. She was already nauseated, and the bus hadn't even left the depot.

"One for you?" He asked the quiet boy.

The boy said nothing.

"That seat taken?"

The boy who looked like a god edged past Freya and claimed the other window seat in the back row. As he passed her, Freya noticed he smelled faintly of honey. He carefully stashed his gear on the ground at his feet. Up close, she could see the small mole above his left eye. The flaw somehow made him even more perfect.

Several other kids climbed onto the bus, all sitting as close to the front as possible. The girl who'd tapped her way through the lounge was last to board. She strode past all the seats, slinging her sack down on the cushion next to Freya. As the coach pulled away, she took her seat, placing her hands on the row in front of her. The floor vibrated as she tapped out a routine. Freya was annoyed but she kept her mouth shut. She didn't want to alienate anyone on the bus, and the god-like guy on the girl's other side was actually moving along to the beat. Clearly she was being overly sensitive.

Freya watched as Dublin rolled past. Despite her queasy stomach, she was excited to leave the city. She had a faint recollection of car trips into the countryside when she was younger. Before the twins. Da had turned the radio loud and he and Mam sang along with old songs from the 90's. It was hard to believe there'd been a time when Mam was actually happy. Sometimes Freya wondered if she herself had ever been happy. She thought so, but she wasn't quite sure.

In no time at all they were among the fields, cruising past pubs and the clutches of smokers gathered on the pavements out front. Sheep and the occasional donkey stood by the roadside, as if watching them pass. Everyone on the bus was surprisingly quiet. Most likely nervous, Freya thought, although she herself was now quite relaxed.

The girl in the green St. Dymphna shirt strode down the aisle of the bus, a large white sack in her hands. She stopped in front of Freya's knees and held up her bag.

"Your mobiles. And any other electronic devices you've got. Drop them in the sack."

She reached past Freya and nudged the god-like boy, who was still gazing out of the window.

The boy took out one ear bud.

"Your phone. Now. In the sack."

He shook his head. "No way. I've the newest model. You'll not get it."

She reached out her hand. "I didn't ask if you wanted to give it to me. For the next two months, I'm the boss of you. That means you will do what I say. Or things could be very unpleasant."

Freya held her breath.

They glared at each other for a moment, before the god-boy dropped his phone into the bag.

"Just know you'll be buying me a new one if there's so much as a scratch."

"Ha! I'd like to see you make that happen," she replied.

The other four surrendered their devices. Freya was careful to lay her phone gently atop the pile, so she didn't damage anyone else's mobile. She had no money to front the costs of any repairs. Freya never had any money.

A moment later the guy with the whistle came down the aisle. He had his own sack, only his was brown.

"Wallets. And in the off chance any of you have bank cards, I'll be taking those as well."

"We're going to be prisoners," the boy with the sweets muttered.

Quinn's back went stiff. With no phones and no money, the guy with the sweets was right. They were captive.

THREE

Quinn watched the guy with the whistle make his way up the aisle. Although he was super thin, he was ripped. His muscles were visible through his shirt. He also had an uncanny sense of balance. Even though the bus was lurching about, he remained centered. The guy was a machine. Half way up the aisle, he stopped, as though he'd just remembered something. He turned around and glared at the dark haired boy in the last row.

"You," he called out to the boy in the back row with the sweets. "What did you say?"

"Nothing." The boy's voice shook.

"That's right. You said, you say, nothing. We'll have no arguments whatsoever. We are the law around here." He shook his head. "You'd think you'd know better. It's crossing your authority figures that's landed you lot in this predicament."

Freya frowned. He sounded exactly like her mother. Mam was forever chiding Freya for "crossing her" every time she offered any opinion.

Green shirt, as Freya began to think of him, was a nightmare. Everyone watched as he glanced down at the wallets in the bag and smirked. He was clearly aware he had an audience, and he was enjoying his performance. He looked up, a nasty smile on his lean face.

"Didn't I see you with a bag of sweets?"

By now everyone was listening. The "campers" in the front half of the bus had their necks craned so they could watch what promised to be an ugly showdown. Freya held her breath. The girl next to her stopped tapping on the seatback.

The boy shook his head.

"Aye, I'm certain of it. You can't fool me," He said in a low voice.

Everyone seemed to hear the threat in his tone. Except the boy with the sweets, who was staring at him defiantly.

"Give 'em here."

"No."

"I said, drop them in the bag." He strode down the aisle, holding up his sack.

Reluctantly the boy reached into his bag and retrieved the sweets, which he tossed into the bag. "I'll get them back, right?"

"Turkish delight. My favorite," Green shirt replied.

As soon as he was gone back up the aisle, Freya turned to her seatmate. Although he'd acted brave, his hands were shaking.

"I'm really sorry. What a jerk."

"My da's going to kill my mam when he sees those sweets are missing. I was only going to eat a few."

Freya shifted uncomfortably in her seat. She'd thought the boy's father looked rather nasty in the departures hall.

The boy nodded. "They're very dear. Da stocks them by the till just so no one can pocket them. We've a takeaway curry shop that also carries some sweets."

"The Right Rice," Freya replied.

"You know it?"

"I've walked past many times. I have to push my sisters around town when Mam's … not feeling well."

"Sisters." He rolled his eyes, although Freya could tell he wasn't actually annoyed. "I've one as well. Total nightmare. She's my parents' favorite child. Which is kind of ironic as most Indians favor their sons. But not in my family. It's all Chaman, why can't you be more like Chaman. I swear that girl doesn't just walk on water, she's created the seas where my parents are concerned."

"We've the same parents, then." The guy with the pricey phone nodded. "For me it's times four. My older brothers and sisters, oh so perfect twenty-four seven. It's like I don't exist. I'm Quinn."

"Freya."

"Ravi."

The girl beating out the pattern was still caught in her own world. Quinn touched her arm. "We're exchanging names here, what's yours?"

Her blue eyes were glassy. She was clearly in her own world. "Maisie."

Everyone turned to the boy hunched against the window.

"Name?" Ravi asked.

The boy didn't reply.

"It's going to be very hard to be alone," Ravi said.

Clearly he hoped this would coax the boy to speak, but he just looked out the window. Ravi looked at the others and shrugged.

Freya leaned back against her seat. The leather was surprisingly comfortable. The bus had settled into a rhythmic cruising speed. Next to her, the girl with the big hair was softly beating out a dance routine that gently shook the floor. Freya took the first deep breath of the day. At some point, she wasn't quite sure how long it had been, she felt the bus slow. She must have fallen asleep, for the next thing she knew the bus was passing signs for Galway.

"Almost there," Ravi said, his voice shaky.

Freya sat up straight. Quinn and the quiet boy were both napping. Maisie was still working on some sort of routine in her head, although she'd stopped tapping the back of the seat in front of her after the girl who was sitting there complained. (Freya did remember hearing the girl telling Maisie off in a rather ominous tone.) She gazed out the window. Galway looked like a storybook come to life, with its colorful shops and pubs and the sea glistening in the background. It was very exciting to see something so different than her dreary block of flats. Freya hoped that somehow the St. Dymphna campers would be allowed to make a stop.

But it was not to be. The bus rolled through town. Almost an hour later, they arrived at Rossaveal port.

"Grab your gear," the green shirts called. "Leave nothing behind on the bus. You'll not have a chance to retrieve any errant items."

Everyone was groggy from the long bus trip. Bags and jackets and water bottles were hauled down from the small overhead shelf and pulled up from the sticky floor.

"Where are we?" Maisie asked.

"Ferry to Inis Mor," the girl in the green shirt called out.

Freya frowned. There was no way the girl could have heard Maisie, yet these minders seemed to have super powers. They were able to anticipate everything everyone said.

They stumbled off the bus and onto the ferry. Once more Freya's stomach was queasy, but she quickly forgot her discomfort at the sight of the vast water. She'd begged her mother to ride the hydrofoil from Dun Laoghaire to Holyhead, but Mam had always said no. Freya was very excited to take a boat ride.

Ten minutes later, they were off, crossing the water. The sea was much rougher than anyone had anticipated. The ferry lurched to and fro. The sharp wind slashed their faces. Freya clutched the rails with an iron grip. She knew she'd have no chance of surviving if she fell overboard. She could barely keep her head above water in a bathtub. Ravi held his hand to his mouth. Several other kids from the bus got sick.

The Cliff of Moher glistened in the distance. As they approach the Aran Island of Inis Mor, limestone slabs, vivid green patches of grass and low stone walls folded out across a desolate island that looked as if it had been thrown from the heavens. A clutch of white farmhouses stood on the horizon. The ferry slid into the dock. A handful of people clapped. Only after the boat was tied did Freya release her hands. She was enchanted.

"It looks like we're at the end of the world."

"You can say that again." Quinn pointed at two wild horses galloping in the distance.

As they walked along the dock, the signs were written in Irish.

"Can't seem to master that language, no matter how I try. My mam keeps forgetting to call it Irish, which doesn't help."

"I didn't know we would be in the Gaeltacht," Maisie said as another cold wind whipped their cheeks. She pulled her jumper up around her neck.

"Fall in line," the guy with the green shirt commanded.

They took up their positions at the rear of the group.

"This lot is the self-appointed cool kids gang," the girl with the green shirt said.

Freya had been called a lot of things, but cool wasn't one of them. Although she was pretty sure both Maisie and Quinn were part of the popular pack at their schools. Ravi too. But the other kid, the one who didn't like to talk? Surely he had never been part of the in crowd? He looked at Freya and smiled. Clearly, he too was flattered at being labelled cool.

"We're off, straight to St. Dymphna's. There will be no dawdling and no talking to anyone along the way. Understood?"

There was a murmur of assent.

"Not much chance we'll have anyone to speak to anyway, there are less than a thousand residents on this island," Quinn said as they made their way along the narrow road. The pavement was cracked and broken in many places. "Less than your average spread of sea lovers on the strand at Bray."

"Impressive," Maisie said. "You're a walking website."

Quinn scowled.

"No, really, I mean it. I've no head for figures. None at all. It's why I'm here. My mam thinks I need maths. But I'm going to dance, on the stage."

"What will you do when your legs give out?" Ravi asked.

Maisie scowled at him. "Seriously?"

Ravi shrugged. "It's a legitimate question."

"Well, if anything ever happens to me, I'll open my own studio."

"Then you're gonna need maths," Quinn said. "Otherwise people will be robbing you blind."

Maisie turned her face away. They walked on in silence, past some old ruins and a pair of sheep who seemed surprised to see a group trekking by their grazing area.

"Why are you here? You seem like you're Mr. Perfect." Maisie turned and stared at Quinn.

"Thank you for noticing," he replied.

No one said anything for a few minutes. The time dragged on. The girl with the green shirt was walking behind them, no doubt to be sure no one escaped the group, though there was clearly nowhere to go. She was listening to music with ear buds. Most likely from one of their phones.

Freya couldn't stand the silence. She'd always been uncomfortable when it was too quiet because it meant the twins were up to something and she was about to get into trouble.

"I'm here because my mam says I'm always crossing her. She makes me call my da every day at his office – he's a banker – and they always say he's with a customer. She never believes me. So I have to call back again. When I finally get off the phone, she says my father left because I'm difficult. Never mind that she's a nightmare and my sisters are horrid."

"I'm sorry Freya," Maisie said.

"Thanks."

"My parents are afraid I'm never going to live up to potential," Ravi said. "The whole 'we didn't come to this country only to watch you fail, don't you appreciate all of our sacrifices?' immigrant kid nightmare. Yes, I do, but I thought coming to Ireland meant I could be myself. Make my own way, not follow in their tracks. If they'd have been keen on having my whole life led by some stupid traditions, they should have left me in India."

"What do you want to do?" Maisie asked.

"Art. I love to draw."

"Cool."

They passed the last house on the horizon. A stretch of desolate road led around the corner. The sea shimmered below, sending sprays of salt water into the air.

"I'm like you, Ravi. The big disappointment," Quinn said.

"Misfits."

They all turned, startled. The quiet boy had spoken. He nodded his head.

"Misfits," he repeated. "We are the misfits."

Quinn laughed. "I think our man here's called it. What's your name, fellow misfit?"

"Tadgh."

The girl with the green shirt stepped between Freya and Ravi.

"No more dawdling. The sun will be down by the time we get to St. Dymphna's. You'll struggle to make a fire."

Make a fire? Maisie and Freya looked at each other.

"Make a fire? She's having one over on us, right?" Freya asked.

"I'm not so sure," Maisie said, pointing at a spot in the distance.

Next to the cliff's edge, above the crashing sea, was a fenced encampment.

"It looks like a prison," Ravi said.

Quinn ran ahead to the front of the line. He grabbed the sleeve of the guy in the green shirt.

"Look here, this is enough. My parents would never have agreed to send me to a place like this. It's uncivilized. I demand to have my mobile."

Green shirt laughed. "Do you hear that, Brie?" He called to the girl in the green shirt. "Fancy boy here believes his parents didn't sign him up for this."

"Right then, everyone just hold up. I usually wait until we're officially on campus to do this, but seeing as the St. Dymphna's sign is within sight, I'll make an exception." She began to reach into her bag. "On second thought, no exceptions. That's what the lot of you are always thinking you deserve. You, my posh little pal, will wait your turn. Come on, keep trekking."

Quinn's cheeks were the color of a radish when he rejoined the other misfits. No one said anything while they hiked toward the gate. Freya gazed around as she walked. There were rocks everywhere, and very steep cliffs that led down to the sea. Strange birds flew over their heads, crying before they dove straight down, out of sight. She shivered. For the first time since they'd left Dublin, Freya was afraid. She liked the others from the back of the bus – the misfits, as Tadgh called them- but what of the others with them? Who knew why they were at St. Dymphna's? Freya knew there were kids her age already setting fires in rubbish cans and knocking old people down for kicks. And clearly the minders in the green shirts were a bit sadistic. They were all alone, out here, trapped on the edge of an island, no mobile phones or way to call for help.

All fifty "campers" fell silent as they made their way to the gate. An enormous stone statue of a woman stood in front of them. Her long fingers were wrapped around a string of rosary beads and a cross. Above her head was a sign that read "St. Dymphna's Holiday Academy" in bold script. As though it was one of the spots where you went with a caravan for summer holidays.

"She was martyred by her father," Freya said quietly.

"No!"

Freya nodded.

Maisie was horrified.

"He cut off her head."

"So our families, our supposed 'loved ones' have sent us to a camp on a deserted island …."

"Exactly."

Maisie reached for Freya's hand. She squeezed her fingers for a moment. Freya was relieved. She had an ally.

After all the campers had entered the property, a wire fence was hastily thrown up by some workers who seemed to come out of nowhere.

"We're trapped," Ravi whispered.

"Right then, I promised you I'd share with you the

program that," the girl with the green shirt scanned the crowd, until she focused on Quinn, "Your parents chose. Let me read from the consent forms, so there are no misunderstandings."

She pulled a form from her bag and read, "For the next two months, your child, or ward, will be surrendered to the custody of St. Dymphna's Holiday Academy in order that he/she may learn the skills necessary to become a functioning member of society."

"That's harsh," Maisie said, "We're already functional members of society."

Green shirt girl held up her hand. "No talking. You don't want to be sent to the isolation tent."

No one was sure if she was joking.

"We – let me introduce myself, I'm Brie, your chief camp counselor. This here is Seamus, your other head counselor. We will be joined by Lexie, Hannah and Owen."

Three other green shirts appeared out of nowhere and stood next to Brie and Seamus.

"For the next eight weeks, you will do what we say, when we say it, without question."

Freya's throat caught. Brie sounded just like her mother.

"I don't get it," Maisie whispered. "What are we going to be doing?"

Brie looked over at Maisie. Once again it seemed like she had an abnormal ability to know what they were all saying and thinking.

"Look around, will you? What do you see?"

"Caravans. Tents. A fire pit," someone shouted.

"That's right. Surprise! This is a wilderness camp."

"My shoes!" Maisie looked down at her feet. As usual she was wearing shoes suitable for breaking into a step routine. Of course they didn't have the taps attached, but they might as well have, for they were totally unfit for anything but a dance studio.

"I've a communal basket of supplies for those of you not suitably outfitted for treks in the wilderness and team building across the hinterlands so to speak."

Freya perked up her ears. Trekking in the wild was just the sort of adventure she'd been hoping to have one day.

Maisie groaned. "If I don't wear something fitted to my feet, I'll get bunions or plantar or one of the other show stoppers."

Freya frowned. Maisie was beginning to seem awfully high maintenance.

"Right then, chop chop, let's have at it. You have already been assigned your bunks. The board beyond the fire pit has the bunk assignments posted. Pass by, note your cabin, drop your gear on your bunk and be here in fifteen minutes."

They looked at each other.

"Don't worry, we're a team," Tadgh whispered.

Freya felt better.

Until she saw the place where she'd be living for the next two months.

FOUR

St. Dymphna's was founded in an era when children were to be seen and not heard. Generations of "at risk" Irish teenagers had been sent to the remote spot at the edge of Inis Mor to cleanse them of what their culture considered their wrongs. Although the standards had changed over the years – the use of corporal punishment was now no longer permitted, and mental health care was given if needed – the principles remained the same. The "campers" as they were called were to be broken down like building kits, to be reassembled in a totally new and different form.

The holiday academy had always been based on the belief that rigorous physical exercise and exposure to the elements was character building. For many years only the counselors had access to indoor plumbing and electricity. Eventually, concessions had been made. Bunk beds replaced the sleeping mats that had been laid on the rough floors of the cabins in earlier days. The rudimentary exercise equipment had been replaced to some extent. However, St. Dymphna's would never be confused with a posh gym, a dance studio or a top drawer holiday camp.

Like much of Inis Mor, the campus featured old Christian ruins. The main house, where the staff stayed, was a sturdy stone building that would easily withstand the howling of the wind and lashing rain that was so much a part of the Aran Islands. The cabins, or quarters for the campers, were a lot more primitive. Besides the wooden bunk beds, scratchy wool blankets, rough floors, very basic plumbing and bare light bulbs hanging from the ceilings on thin chords, the cabins also featured the smell of mold and fear.

Everyone was scared. Even those who pretended otherwise.

Freya was dismayed to discover she and Maisie were not in the same cabin. Slowly Freya watched Maisie disappear into a cabin with girls who smiled at each new arrival. She was afraid she'd have no such luck. She was right. It was inevitable there would be nasty, spiteful girls in the group, but Freya was still surprised to learn they'd all be her cabin mates, especially since they all seemed to know each other already. Even though Freya's seven bunkmates were an odd number, she'd no hope of fitting in to their crew. There was no possibility of being the eighth member of the clique. They were all loud and bossy. Each one seemed to be the type who hung out on Grafton Street with their parents' credit cards on Saturdays. Freya wondered why they were here.

Freya wandered outside. Maisie was stepping out of the girls' cabin on the other side of the fire pit, wearing ridiculous trainers that were clearly two sizes too big. She must have gotten them from the communal supply basket.

"Hey, I've extra trainers if you want to give them a go."

"Ah that's grand, you saved my life. Thanks a mil." Maisie followed her back inside the cabin.

Freya's bunkmates glared at her and Maisie as she rummaged through her bag. She had one good pair of trainers, which she handed to Maisie. Better to have a few blisters or maybe wet feet if rain seeped in through the hole in the sole in her spare pair.

"You sure?" Maisie looked doubtful.

"Positive."

Quinn, Ravi and Tadgh were outside when they got back to the fire pit, Maisie's feet comfortable in Freya's treasured trainers.

"I'm all set to do a runner," Maisie whispered.

Freya laughed. "Not sure how that would work out. Do you think they've guards?"

"Maybe."

"From what I've heard, we'd be begging to be let back in if we were lost out here," Quinn said.

"Seriously?" Ravi shook his head. "This island looks pretty harmless to me."

"Haunted. The wormhole," Tadgh said.

They all turned to him.

"What is a wormhole?" Maisie asked.

"Only the coolest thing ever. It's a way to travel through time. To another dimension. Like Tadgh said, there's supposedly one right here, on Inis Mor." Quinn nodded.

"I still don't get it. It's a hole in the ground, the size of a worm? Or there are worms?"

"No worms!" Quinn practically shouted.

Two girls nearby looked their direction. Ravi, Tadgh, Freya and Maisie moved closer.

Quinn looked at Tadgh. "Do you want to tell her?"

Tadgh shook his head.

"Right then. Maisie, a wormhole is a door to another world. It's like the hole a worm digs inside of an apple. A quick way to move from one place to another. It's a place where anything can happen...."

Maisie whimpered. "I still don't get it!"

"It's a scientific principle," Freya said. "An attempt to explain Einstein's theory of relativity. A way to unify electromagnetic fields and gravity."

"So you can slip through time," Maisie said.

"Exactly."

"That is the coolest thing I've ever heard! Sign me up, how do we get there? Defying gravity – if I could learn to do that I'd be the most unique dancer on the planet."

Quinn frowned. "I'm not sure it works quite like that…."

"Killjoy," Maisie stuck out her tongue.

Quinn held up his hands. "Hey who am I to define the laws of physics? For all we know you could be dancing upside down on these cliffs if we could find the thing. Of course it's not just finding it, it's getting inside the wormhole. Otherwise it's just another hole in the ground."

"I know," Tadgh began as a whistle blew.

"Line up. Now! Our first challenge is on. That's right, charges, you'll be earnin' your meals. Challenges and chores. Chores and challenges."

Challenges and chores. Chores and challenges. It became the mantra for the next week as the St. Dymphna's Holiday Academy attendees were put through their paces. They went on long hikes. Raced over hurdles. Cooked and cleaned up meals for everyone at the academy, on a rotating chore list. Mopped the rough floors of the dining hall. Swept the embers from the fire pit where they gathered at night, beneath the stars. It was exhausting, yet somehow each camper became more relaxed.

Quinn had never imagined he'd be able to sleep in such shabby quarters. He'd been camping, plenty of times, with his brothers and Scouts Ireland. Yet as rustic as the tents and cabins he'd stayed in had been, this was the first time he was constantly snagging his clothes and his flesh on the splintered wood of the rough bunk. He'd taken the top because he'd always been relegated to the bottom by his brothers. And he had a feeling that Tadgh, who was a bit clumsy, would have trouble with the climb.

Tadgh still didn't speak much, which was fine as Ravi talked enough for the pair of them. On and on he went about his drawings and his school and how difficult it was when people came into the shop for a takeaway without any money. They begged to take their curry on credit, which Ravi always allowed and which infuriated his father. No doubt the hundreds of free curries he'd given away over the years had something to do with him being sent to the holiday academy.

At least they were together. Quinn had pitied Freya, something he rarely did, when he saw the girls she'd been stuck with for roommates. He knew enough about his sisters' lives to realize she was going to be mocked for her accent, her cheap clothes and her overly eager desire to talk with everyone she encountered.

Freya actually did better than anyone expected, for she was enjoying time away from the twins. It wasn't that she didn't love her sisters, rather she hated how they were the stars of her life. At least at St. Dymphna's she didn't have to listen constantly, panic filling her throat every time the lounge was too quiet, certain Nora and Allie were a half step from catastrophe. She hated the fact that her cabin mates didn't include her in the nightly gossip after the lightbulb was turned out, but she was used to it. Freya had never had much time for friends. That was the unexpected bonus of being at St. Dymphna's. Maisie, Quinn, Ravi and Tadgh waited for her every night at the fire pit. Freya looked up at the moon and smiled. She was happy.

FIVE

"Take it outside, Maisie!"

The tiny lodge reverberated with the shuffling echoes of her constantly tapping feet. She'd stopped worrying about whether her arches would fall if she tapped in Freya's trainers, and begun to concentrate on her routines. It was difficult keeping a beat, especially when the other girls deliberately pounded the floor at odd intervals.

Maisie rolled her eyes. She was so sick of her cabin mates' complaints about her dancing. Didn't they know how important it was to keep up with her routines? If only she had known her phone was to be taken away, she would have written the steps down on a sheet of paper so she'd have them on hand in case she got nervous. Maisie tended to forget things when she was upset. Her mother called it "Maisie's Mush Mind," which wasn't kind but was an accurate description of the muddled mess that seemed to take over her head whenever she had to concentrate for too long. It was completely unfair, expecting her to remember the elaborate routines she was used to recording. She was already losing precious studio time. She'd be lucky to qualify for the feis at the rate things were going.

"Give it up girl, you've two left feet," Andrea said, tossing her pillow at Maisie. "Seriously, who do you think you are? This isn't your flat. You've no right to subject the rest of us to your awful rhythms."

Maisie was shocked. No one had ever accused her of being uncoordinated. Were they right? Was she losing her touch? For years she'd been confident she was the best, but she'd always known she could be toppled at any time. New anger at her parents rose in her chest as she considered the possibility they'd sent her to St. Dymphna's so she would fail at dancing. It was so unfair. They should have sent her to dance camp. Or at least someplace where she would have access to her shoes. She looked down at Freya's trainers, with the stain on the left toe and the slight hole near the laces. Maybe she was ruining her feet. She walked outside.

Ravi was sitting against a tree, a tiny square of paper in hand. He didn't look up as she approached.

"What're you doing?"

He held up his drawing of the Cliffs of Moher.

"Very cool. You've captured their pock marks."

"What?"

Maisie pointed at the hills. "See? They look like a face full of spots."

Ravi laughed. "Not what I was expecting."

Maisie sat down across from him. "None of this is what I anticipated. I don't get the point. Why am I here? It seems all they're doing is getting us in shape which, hello, I am already fit. Well maybe also teaching about being part of a team. But I already know how to do that. My studio goes to the feis as a troupe."

"You compete together? Really? I thought it was every girl for herself."

"There's team stuff and individual."

"Cool." Ravi looked at Maisie's hair. Her curls were sticking out at all angles. "Your hair is, I bet you don't have to wear a wig."

Maisie touched her hair. "Yeah, I've the curls to pull it off." She sighed. "When do you think they'll let us have some fun?"

Ravi shrugged. "I'm enjoying myself."

Maisie studied Ravi. He seemed to be the kind of person who could have a good time no matter where he was, or what he was doing. "Lucky you."

"Show me one of your steps."

"What?"

"Yeah," Ravi stood. "It'd make my sister green with envy if I came home knowing a dance."

"You're on. But first, take off those boots before you break a toe."

Ravi kicked off his boots and stood. "Pity I don't have a wig."

Maisie laughed. "You eejit. Come on, brush your right foot straight out in front of you."

Freya saw Maise and Ravi. They were beneath a large tree, atop one of the slabs of limestone that seemed to pop up out of the ragged ground when least expected. She looked to her left. Quinn was just coming out of his cabin. She headed in his direction.

"Are they dancing?" Quinn peered into the distance.

Freya followed his gaze. Maisie and Ravi were now atop the limestone, brushing their feet in a steady motion.

"Sure looks like it."

"Aye, they've gone mad from the boredom." Quinn took a deep breath. "I've been far too tired to be bored."

"Same. Where's Tadgh?"

"Inside the cabin."

"Do you know what day it is?"

Quinn shook his head. "I've no idea. You?"

"Not a clue."

Brie strode out of the stone lodge where the staff slept and ate, polishing off the last of a chocolate bar. Freya's mouth watered at the sight. They'd been given a strict vegetarian diet. Except every third day, or perhaps it was every fourth, Freya had lost count, when a bit of chicken had been added into the midday meal. Lexie had explained that the director of St. Dymphna believed that food additives and too much protein were the source of many behavioral issues, so they would not be having anything that was not organic, raw or vegan. Quinn had asked about honey. The counselors said it was strictly forbidden as it was an animal by-product. Quinn was very pleased, although lots of the others were griping.

Brie was joined by Lexie, who was everyone's favorite counselor. Where the others were hard, Lexie was soft. She was the one people confided in when they'd reached their edge. When the races and the competitions and the unplugged nature of their days became overwhelming. Rumor had it she'd even lent one of the girls in the third cabin a blanket when she'd struggled to sleep in the cold night air, although that had never been proven. Lexie waved at the campers and smiled before she blew her whistle. A moment later, everyone had gathered on the craggy ground outside the stone lodge.

"Right then, not sure I should say this, but you've earned a free afternoon. Is that okay with you, Brie?"

Brie paused a moment before nodding her head in agreement.

A round of applause loud enough to be heard on the mainland erupted.

"Pipe it down, you'll wake the dead. Back here by half six or they'll be no more liberty passes."

"What shall we do?" Freya's eyes were wide.

"The wormhole," Tadgh said.

"It's just an urban legend," Maisie said. She looked at the others. "Right?"

"We'll find out."

"Have you any idea where it is?"

Quinn nodded. "We'll have to be careful. We can leave the grounds through the side facing the sea. No one will suspect."

Freya shivered. "Isn't it a straight drop down onto the rocks?"

"No, there's a good ten meters."

"That's not much cushion."

"More than you need."

"Here's the plan, we head for the far left corner, meet on the other side. I'm pretty sure I know where the serpent's lair lies."

"What is that?"

"Another name for the wormhole."

Twenty minutes later were gathered on the other side of the wire fence. Quinn had been right, there was a gap in the barrier. All they'd had to do was walk to the other side.

Maisie inhaled. "Freedom tastes delicious."

"It's the sea air," Tadgh said.

Maisie smiled. "Whatever it is, I'm not complaining. So where's this lair?"

Quinn looked up at the sky, then out at the horizon. "That direction."

"What are you, a human compass?" Freya asked.

"Something like that."

They set out along the craggy path. Tall wild grass jutted up between bits of limestone.

"My feet," Maisie groaned.

"It's going to make you that much more agile," Ravi offered.

The sea stretched out below them, every shade of green and blue. The stony remains of old buildings and a handful of white farmhouses popped up in the distance.

"I swear some of the others have Stockholm Syndrome," Freya said as they walked. "They're not even leaving the cabin. And they're all about the rules. I don't know why they're even here."

"Yeah, seems like their purpose is to make our lives miserable," Maisie said. "Although I think they're in it for the sweets. I'm sure that the ones tattling on me for dancing at night or heading to the loo after hours are being paid off with Jaffa Cakes and orange sodas."

"Do you really think so?" Tadgh was wistful.

He sounded like a small boy. Maisie didn't want to disappoint him, so she said, "Nah, I'm sure they're suffering as well."

"Hope so," Tadgh replied.

They all laughed.

As they rounded the bend they came upon a dilapidated house, half set in a hollow.

"All Hallows Eve has come early," Quinn said. He leaned forward, then smiled. "Listen."

A faint buzz filtered up from the hollow. Quinn followed it.

"Quinn?"

He disappeared from their sight. They looked at each other, then climbed into the hollow.

Quinn was standing in front of a beehive. "Bombus muscorum," he said. "I never thought I'd see one."

Freya stepped forward and gazed into the hive, which was enclosed in mesh. "It looks like a flying spider."

"Yeah, they're pretty unusual for bees," Quinn said. "I love the amber."

"Very cool." Ravi grabbed a piece of paper and pencil stub from his pocket and made a quick sketch.

"I don't know why the hive is in mesh." Quinn frowned.

"Who cares why, at least we're not to be stung," Ravi said.

"Maybe someone's using them for honey," Maisie said.

"I don't think so," Quinn replied.

A huge clap of thunder clattered across the sky. When she was little, Freya's father used to tell her the gods were bowling in the heavens whenever thunder rumbled.

"We've got about five minutes," Quinn said.

They scrambled back up the hill. Freya turned over her shoulder for one last look at the hollow and its desolate, crumbling cottage. A woman with wild white hair was standing next to the hive. She waved.

"Did you see that?"

Quinn nodded.

A moment later the clouds opened. By the time they reached St. Dymphna's they were so soaked they were actually glad to be back on the grounds.

Brie watched from the deep staff porch as they scrambled back to their cabins. She was standing with Lexie and Hannah, the two counselors who didn't ever speak. Maisie was afraid they knew the five of them had left the grounds. Then again, maybe that would be a reason to be expelled from St. Dymphna's. She'd have the chance to return to the dance studio for the summer.

Maybe they should act up more often.

SIX

Freya had never had a boyfriend. A lot of the other girls at school held hands with boys, sometimes even hanging around the alleys after dark with them. Freya had never had the time, since she was always babysitting. And she'd never been one of those girls other boys looked at. Rather she was far too often "one of the guys," which was code for good at maths and science. She'd like plenty of boys over the years, but no one had ever noticed her. Until Ravi.

She'd caught him staring at her a few times since they'd arrived at St. Dymphna's. Once when she was finishing her fruit cup, before she had dish duty. He'd been sitting across the sloppy dining room with Quinn and Tadgh and two other boys whose names she couldn't remember. She felt the blood rush to her cheeks when she saw him looking. Her face turned the shade of a beet when he smiled at her across the room. She'd smiled slightly, then turned back to dragging her spoon across the bottom of the chipped bowl.

The other girls at school often ignored boys who liked them. Freya figured she'd try that strategy. Hiding her feelings was something she'd never tried before. Maybe if she'd been better about camouflaging how she felt she wouldn't have been sent to St. Dymphna's. Then again, she was having the best summer of her life.

"I think Ravi likes you."

Freya hadn't noticed the girl who had the bunk across from hers sit down. The girl looked at Ravi and made a big kissing face. Freya's cheeks became even hotter. She got up and walked away, her back to the mean girl. It took everything she had not to tell off the girl – Daphne, she thought her name was – but there was no way she wanted to land in the solitary space reserved for those who broke the rules. Those kids didn't get any free time.

Ravi shook his head. He pitied Freya, stuck with all the nasty girls. He'd heard them slagging off everyone one afternoon. They were brutal. He wanted to say something comforting to Freya, but given the circumstances, he didn't know how. So he went in search of Tadgh.

"The others in Freya's cabin, they're wretched."

Tadgh nodded.

"They make her feel awful."

All of his life, or at least for as long as he could remember, Tadgh had wanted to be the hero. To swoop in, save the day and have everyone pat him on the back. To be the one everyone turned to, instead of away from. Finally, he had his chance.

"I'll do it."

"Do what?" Ravi was puzzled.

"Save Freya."

"No! Freya doesn't need saving."

Tadgh didn't understand. Why would Ravi have told him about a problem, unless he wanted a solution? Tadgh's imposing build and unusual ways had always meant people were somewhat afraid of him. He was certain he could frighten Freya's cabin mates into leaving her alone.

Ravi studied Tadgh. He resembled Speckles, the dog that used to come into the curry shop with its owner, before Mr. McHannerty died. The dog was always a bit guarded, never allowing anyone but Mr. McHannerty to touch him. When the old man collapsed on the street in front of the shop late one afternoon, Speckles had not allowed the anyone to come close enough to Mr. McHannerty to render aid. The entire community watched in horror as the old man writhed on the pavement and eventually passed away, without ever receiving the CPR that might have saved his life. Speckles stood guard by the body, until a garda had trapped him with a net and Mr. McHannerty was finally carted away.

"It's cool you want to help," Ravi said. "You can be Freya's friend. She'd like that, she needs people to listen to instead of those eejits she's bunking with."

"I can do that."

"Good man."

Tadgh wondered, should he approach Freya now?

While he was debating with himself, Freya appeared in the distance, brushing dirt from her jeans. She was joined by Maisie, who as always seemed to dance rather than walk.

They looked over at the boys, then turned to each other.

"How many years have you been dancing?"

"Since I could walk."

"Must be nice."

"Have you never done a lesson?"

Freya scoffed. "I wish! Not in my house, there's no money and no time. My mam has me playing mother to my twin sisters. I'm barely able to grab a moment to myself."

"Ah, that's a shame." Maisie tugged on one of her long curls. "Do you want to learn a step or two?"

"I'm far too clumsy."

"No such thing. You should see me, half the time I'm trippin' up the stairs at home. Come on, there's a stretch of rock behind the cabins that's good as a stage."

Freya appreciated that she wouldn't be able to be seen by the girls from her cabin, or anyone else at St. Dymphna's. She had always been self-conscious about how little control she seemed to have over her arms and legs.

"Follow me," Maisie said, brushing her right foot against the ground.

Freya picked up her right foot. To her amazement, she was able to copy Maisie's movement without any problem.

"You got it!"

They continued with the lesson. An hour later, Freya, who had always longed to dance, had mastered a simple routine. And Maisie had made a new friend. Later that night, when Maisie's cabin mates were slagging off Freya, Maisie told them they should be so lucky to be half as smart.

SEVEN

The founder of St. Dymphna's was a rebellious nun who believed that an idle body was the devil's workspace. The premise of the holiday academy was to impart skills that would keep the "guests" as the staff sarcastically called them constantly on the move. That way they'd be far too exhausted to engage in disruptive behaviors. Old patterns would be broken. The campers would return to their homes literally reassembled, this time all the parts in the right places.

Although she was feeling more confident since she'd begun practicing the simple dance routines Maisie showed her, Freya was still self-conscious about her clumsiness and constantly worried she'd never be chosen for any of the games teams. Quinn made sure she was always one of the first chosen. A natural athlete, both he and Maisie were always first picks.

Most of the time, though, the staff at St. Dymphna's made sure the campers were mixed in randomly. Lexie especially constantly preached about the need to "know all your mates." However, Freya never found the others to be friendly. It was such a relief to have her little crew.

Freya wasn't the only one thrilled to have found friends.

Tadgh was aware that everyone thought he was weird. For as long as he could remember, he'd known he was different from other people. It hadn't taken long to realize they felt the same about him. It wasn't a big problem. In fact, there were times he'd used it to his advantage, especially when he was younger. The teachers in year one had been very sympathetic to his lack of friends. He'd gotten the best seat in class, extra biscuits at the morning tea break and first crack at all the fat books in the library.

But for the last few years, ugly words had been bantered about, words that belonged in medical textbooks, used by his parents, his teachers and, worst of all, his classmates. People talked about him as though Tadgh couldn't hear. Ravi had been horrified at his offer to help Freya, although he wasn't quite sure why scaring her cabin mates would have been so bad. Ravi had given him the wary eye he'd seen for as long as he could remember. And now, Maisie had given him the strange look, the one he'd come to recognize that meant people were afraid of him. He'd have to make an effort. He didn't want to be alone, despite what others thought.

She was on a patch of limestone, tapping out another routine. Tadgh made sure she saw him approach. He didn't want to scare her; so many girls at school complained he snuck up on them, which wasn't true at all. He was just light on his feet. Perhaps he should consider dragging them when he walked.

He sat in the bit of rough wild grass in front of her and watched. She danced for another few minutes. Although he didn't know much about music, he swayed along to the beat.

"Glad you like my steps. I've been working up a new routine." Maisie dropped down on the ground next to him.

"Very cool."

"Thanks." She picked up one of the long green blades and rubbed it between her fingers.

"Mind if I ask you something?"

Tadgh shrugged.

"Why are you here?"

Tadgh didn't reply.

"The rest of us clearly have issues. But you're just shy. Which should not be a crime."

Tadgh willed his eyes not to fill with tears. It was the kindest thing anyone had ever said. He looked down at his feet, his long toes almost bursting out of the sides of his trainers.

"Whatever it is that brought you, I'm glad you're here." Maisie stood up. "I've got to keep moving or I'll forget my steps. It's always the way with a new routine, I'm useless until I've got the muscle memory kicked. Then it's locked in for life."

Tadgh watched as she repeated the steps. As she was midway through the last turn Quinn and Ravi sat down on his right side.

"We have to find the wormhole."

Tadgh was slightly irritated. He was enjoying watching Maisie dance. Feeling a part of things.

"She's so cool," Quinn said quietly.

Tadgh turned to Quinn.

"Don't you think?"

Tadgh smiled. Quinn liked Maisie. It was the first time someone had ever told him about a crush.

"Where is Freya?" Ravi looked around. "She's never in her cabin."

As if sensing she was being called, Freya appeared from behind the other girls' lodge.

"I want to swim," she said quietly when she joined the group. "I've never been in the ocean."

"Swim in these waters? You must be mad. And you'll drown." Ravi's voice shook.

"Not if we find the wormhole." Freya looked at Quinn. "It's self-enclosed, right? And it should be warm."

"I don't think it's safe," Quinn said.

"Well I want to find out. I'm so bored I could cry, and I can't stop thinking about the possibilities. Time travel. Where would you go if you could go anywhere?"

"To the future," Tadgh said. "I want to know, everything turns out okay."

Freya patted his arm. "Everything is going to be fine."

"I'd like to see dinosaurs," Ravi said. "Feel the earth shake when they walked."

"I'd go inside the jungle. I'd find all the bees no one knows about. What about you Freya?"

"I'm not sure. Although I think it would have to be someplace with no babysitting and no chores." She looked over at Maisie. "I think we all know where she'd head. The largest stage in the universe."

They all laughed.

They couldn't believe their luck. Another free afternoon. Although Quinn wanted to visit the hive again, Freya, Ravi, Maisie and Tadgh convinced him that a trip to the serpent's lair was in order. Luckily Quinn had a keen enough sense of geography that he knew roughly where the wormhole lay.

"It's near the fort," he said as they walked along the path, St. Dymphna's at their backs.

"Dun Aonghassa."

They walked along the rugged road, once again alone.

"I still think this place feels like we've arrived at the end of the world," Ravi said.

"Agreed," Freya chimed in. "Especially with all the weird birds here."

"I think that's 'cause we're city people," Ravi replied. "We're not used to nature."

"But we've Phoenix Park," Tadgh said.

They all smiled.

Even though they never discussed it among themselves, they all knew something was a bit unusual about Tadgh. Quinn and Ravi had taken to shielding him from the others in their cabin, which Tadgh rightfully understood to mean they were his friends. He had never been so happy.

"Look!" Maisie pointed.

Massive limestone rocks led down to the sea. In the middle lay one perfect stone rectangle. Water foamed inside its borders.

"It looks like a swimming pool. Surely someone's made this?"

"No," Quinn said. "It's all natural."

The jade waters swirled. Beyond the mossy limestone, the open sea crashed.

"I was just kidding about swimming," Freya said.

"'course we know you're joking," Ravi said. "You'd have to have a death wish to go in there. You'd be dragged out to sea in no time. And battered against the rocks."

"What a way to go." Maisie shivered.

"It's fantastic," Tadgh said. "Let's climb down. See it up close."

"No way. It's too dangerous," Ravi said.

"The Red Bull diving contest was held here in 2017. Thousands of people were on these rocks and they lived to tell the tale," Quinn said.

Freya bit her lip. She'd always longed for an adventure. However, she wasn't a strong swimmer. What if she was somehow pulled out to sea? She never should have made the joke about swimming.

Maisie surveyed the slick, uneven rocks. Moss grew along many of the sides, which would make them extra slippery. "I don't know, what if I hurt my feet?"

Quinn held out his hand. "I'll hold onto you the entire time. You'll not fall."

Reluctantly, Maisie took his hand.

They started carefully down the rocks toward the blowhole. Freya, Ravi and Tadgh looked at each other. Surely it was safe? Tadgh nodded. They made their way down to the lower level.

"The serpent's lair," Quinn pronounced as they sat on a wide ledge above the sinkhole.

"Word is a serpent guards the entrance to the underworld…."

Tadgh slid. Ravi leaned forward, trying to hold onto him.

Quinn, Freya and Maisie watched in horror as their friends disappeared into the foaming serpent's lair.

EIGHT

"What do we do?" Maisie was hysterical. "Help! HELP!"

They all screamed, their voices echoing, tears running down their cheeks.

"You two go up to the road. See if you can flag anyone. I'm going after them."

Freya and Maisie both grabbed Quinn's arms.

"No! We can't lose you too."

They laced their hands together and held onto Quinn. He wriggled, but then realized they were right. There was nothing he could do, except keep vigil. A moment later, Freya, who had never been religious, began to pray. Maisie and Quinn joined.

A streak of sun brightened the sky, followed by the sound of splashing. An enormous wave rose up within the rectangle. Ravi and Tadgh were in the middle of the crest. The sea had delivered them from the serpent's lair.

"They're back!"

Freya, Maisie and Quinn rushed toward the edge of the limestone rocks. Ravi and Tadgh disappeared again. Freya felt as if she'd been punched. But a second later, they were climbing out of the wormhole. They pulled themselves onto the rocks, then lay back, clearly exhausted. A moment later, Ravi turned and waved.

"I'm going down to help them up," Quinn said. "They've got to be weak."

"Careful," Maisie said.

Quinn nodded over his shoulder.

Maisie wrapped her arm around Freya's shoulder. They huddled together, holding their breath, as Quinn carefully climbed down to where Ravi and Tadgh were now sunning themselves. He turned around and gave them a thumbs up.

"I thought they were goners for sure." Maisie shivered.

"They must've been scared out of their minds."

The wind was wicked. It seemed to have whipped up out of nowhere, tossing the sea and their hair.

"They must be cold. Very cold."

"Let's get them warmed up."

Maisie frowned. "Do you think we can make it down safely?"

"As long as we hold onto each other."

Carefully they made their way down to the wormhole, where they stripped off their jumpers and laid them on Ravi and Tadgh.

"Thanks a mil," Ravi said.

"I'm just glad you're here," Freya said.

Ravi smiled.

"Awesome," Tadgh said. "Next time, we all go."

Quinn looked at Freya and Maisie. Clearly Tadgh had some issues. There was no way anyone should contemplate going down into the Serpent's Lair.

They all sat on the limestone and watched the waves crash.

"I can't believe you didn't drown," Maisie said. "You two must be strong swimmers."

"And very lucky," Freya added.

Ravi shook his head. "We were protected. Weren't we, Tadgh?"

Tadgh nodded. "The animals took care of us."

Quinn raised his eyebrows. He'd read that people suffering hypothermia had a constellations of symptoms. However, hallucinating wasn't one of them.

"Animals?" Maisie asked.

"The great auks were the best. Letting me hold their flaps, nudging me with their bills…."

Freya frowned. She had read her way through many of the science books on the school library shelves during lunch hour. The great auks, the penguin like bird that did not fly, had been long extinct in Ireland.

"A grey wolf offered to let me ride her back, but I was afraid I was too heavy."

"We need to get you warmed up," Quinn said.

He exchanged worried looks with Freya. Clearly something had happened to Tadgh when they were under the water. Or, perhaps that strangeness he conveyed was indeed a sign he was a bit unhinged.

"Let's get back to St. Dymphna and hot showers," Maisie said.

It took a while but they finally made their way back to the main road, then to the path that led to the holiday academy. Luckily no one was out when they arrived; Freya and Quinn were quite concerned Tadgh would tell his wild tale about auks and grey wolves and perhaps be sent to the infirmary, where rumor had it the doctor was rather adept at shooting errant campers with tranquilizers.

"I'll keep watch," Quinn said quietly to Freya and Maisie.

They nodded their thanks.

"Should we do another dance?" Maisie asked as they walked away from the boys.

Freya bit her lip. “I’m not sure I can concentrate.”

“Exactly,” Maisie said. “You dance when you can’t focus. It brings you back to yourself. Come on, we’ve still an hour before dinner.”

They walked along the path, to a small isolated space, where they danced until Lexie blew the dinner whistle.

NINE

"You've been here for three weeks now, and I must admit, there's been a lot of improvement," Brie said several nights later through her megaphone.

The St. Dymphna's campers were sitting beneath the stars, admiring the night sky.

Freya looked around. The group had shrunken since they'd arrived. One of the girls from her cabin was already gone. Gemma, her name was. She'd gone mad with worry one night, begun pulling her hair from her head and screaming she was going to drop out of school rather than sit for her certs. Lexie had collected her straight away and hauled her off to the counselors' den, where her parents had been called. Rumor was her father had chartered a plane from Dublin for her, although no one could be sure. All they knew was that she was gone.

After Gemma left, a bottom bunk had opened in the cabin. Freya was shocked, and distrustful, when one of the girls offered it to her.

"Ah, they think it's cursed," Maisie had said. "They're sure you'll go next if you sleep in that space. Bad karma and auras and all that. I never believed in any of that myself, even though me granny's quite fond of readin' the tea leaves when her old biddies come to town."

Freya shivered. Unlike Maisie, she wasn't so sure the supernatural didn't exist. The wormhole, for example. Surely there had been some sort of force that returned Tadgh and Ravi to them after they'd disappeared into the sea.

"You've earned another liberty pass as we're want to call it," Brie announced.

Everyone clapped.

"What'll we do?" Maisie asked.

"The wormhole," Tadgh said.

Freya, Maisie and Quinn frowned. Tadgh, who had never been one to talk, now spoke non-stop about endangered animals and his big adventure. The others were worried he'd be considered mad, but he didn't seem to care, since he was used to people dismissing him. His new friends didn't understand.

"The liberty will be in two days' time," Brie announced. "Now hop to it, we've arrows to shoot."

Freya scrambled to her feet. She loved trying out all the different sports on offer at St. Dymphna. Between the dancing and the archery and the running with a baton and the long walks and the runs past the stone ruins that dotted the area, Freya was beginning to fancy herself an athlete. Perhaps she'd even join one of the running groups when she got back to school.

She must be mad. There was no time for hobbies in Freya's life. The moment Freya thought of the outside world she was depressed. Mam and the twins. Even her da. It was all so much. She loved the routine of St. Dymphna. Knowing that every day her hard work would be rewarded by a feeling of accomplishment, instead of complaints about the spots on Nora's jumper or the crumbs on the table. Falling into a deep sleep at night, without being woken by the sound of her mother's sobbing or the twins' fighting. She didn't ever want to leave this place, where for the first time she'd finally felt like her own person. Freya kept that to herself though, since she knew Maisie was still fretting over how far behind she'd be when she finally got back to the dance studio.

Ravi, however, seemed to share her contentment. He was sitting under the tree, drawing, after they finished their archery. Ever since he'd almost drowned, Freya had been overcome with a desire to let him know she liked him, especially since she was sure he felt the same way.

She walked over to him and looked down at his drawing. A grey wolf. He looked up at her and smiled.

"I'm chronicling it all," he said, "So I don't forget what we saw."

Freya forced herself to smile. Clearly she'd misjudged Ravi. He was as batty as Tadgh.

As if he read her mind, Ravi looked into her eyes. "I know what you're thinking. But it's true, I swear. You said you were open to time travel. Why don't you believe me?"

"It sounds insane."

"I know. Believe me, I have always been very rational. But this, it's changed me."

"I don't want to keep you from your drawing."

Freya bit her lip. She had so much to consider. Was it possible there was a time slip? That her friends really had fallen into an era when the animals long gone from Ireland were still alive?

"Hey Ravi, how was everything alive in the water?"

"We weren't under water. Oh sure, at first we were in the sea. But we landed on an island, deep somewhere in the earth's core. At least I think that's where it must be."

Freya nodded. She looked around at the other archers.

Quinn was just shooting his last arrow. The moment he finished she ambled over to him.

"What do you think about all this talk of extinct animals?"

"They definitely think they saw something. It's weird. I don't know why they'd have that impression...."

"Do you think it happened?"

Quinn shrugged. "I don't know. We have internet. Signals fly across the world, through electric magnetic fields we can't see. Who's to say they're not also pitching back in time?"

"I think it would be dangerous to go back."

"Yeah. I want to see the hives."

"Let's do that on the off day."

"Deal."

When the liberty pass day finally arrived, Freya, Maisie, Quinn, Ravi and Tadgh agreed to set off for the hives. Tadgh and Ravi were hoping they'd eventually make their way down to the wormhole, although they didn't share that with the others. They were both certain an alternate world existed, and they couldn't wait to return.

TEN

"You're a human compass," Ravi said to Quinn.

It was impressive. Quinn had them retracing the identical route they'd taken to the hives. They walked through fields of wildflowers and tall grasses. Dodged the stone ruins that jutted from the ground at odd intervals. Avoided the strange crevices that marred the landscape, which was rugged and even more beautiful than they'd remembered. In the distance, the sea was a quilt of green and blue.

Maisie opened her mouth. "I love the way the air on this island tastes. Like an ocean mouthwash."

Freya laughed.

Quinn grew more excited with each step. He missed his hives, and was elated at the idea of seeing other bees. He didn't dare let himself think about what was going on at home.

They could hear the bees as they approached. Only today, they were not alone. A pale, white haired woman with enormous blue eyes, dressed in lacy white clothing that made her look like something out of a steampunk novel or video game, was tending to the far hive. As she watched them approach, drums and some fiddles sounded in the distance.

"Come to see the wee ones, have you?"

"If we can," Quinn said.

"Of course, they're nature's babies, not mine."

They climbed down into the slight hollow. To their great surprise, a number of bees, perhaps three dozen, flew in a circle around the woman's head. She stepped close to the farthest hive and commanded, "Right then, back in you go," and the bees flew back into the hive.

"Did you see that?" Maisie whispered.

"I think," Ravi replied.

"Impressive," Quinn said. "How do you make that happen?"

"I've no idea what you're talking about," the woman said. "I'm Aine. Welcome."

Freya groaned. First Ravi and Tadgh had gone a bit mad after their slip into the wormhole, and now this woman. Perhaps she had been right to fear the west.

"Don't be afraid," Aine said, extending her hand to Freya. "Insects and animals know who to trust."

Freya shook Aine's slender hand.

"How long have you had the hives?" Quinn asked.

"Who can say? I barely remember a time without them. My family's been here for hundreds of years. In this very house."

The derelict home looked like it was about to fall into the earth. The stone wall on the end was coming down, and two of the window panes were propped up against a low hedge, leaving the windows open to the elements.

Aine noticed Freya looking at the house.

"Would you like to have a look 'round inside?"

Freya, like everyone she knew, had been warned of "stranger danger" since she was small. She would never consider going inside the house of someone she didn't know in

Dublin. However, she wasn't alone, and Inis Mor certainly wasn't the city.

"I'd like that."

"Come." Aine headed to the house. She looked back over her shoulder. "The lot of you are welcome."

"I'll mind the bees," Quinn said.

"Fair enough."

The others followed Aine inside. From the exterior they expected to find a ramshackle house with no electricity, perhaps no running water, and certainly no luxuries. They were wrong.

The room with the broken panes turned out to be a sun porch, crowded with rocking chairs, blankets and fat throw pillows.

"My gear for star gazing," Aine said. "You can learn so much about earth from the heavens."

After the sun room came an enormous kitchen, with a black stove that had a small door in the bottom for a fire to be started, six burners and, nearby, a giant oven.

"My da would love this," Ravi said. "He's cooking up curry on two simple gas hobs."

Freya gazed around in wonder. She'd never seen such luxury. Dozens of copper pans, lavender hanging upside down on pegs, embroidered towels, flowerpots full of fresh herbs and a heaving basket of fresh fruits. Colored glass bottles full of liquids, many of them labeled in Irish, lined up neatly under a painting of silver pitcher. Every detail was so perfect it looked like a magazine cover.

The room beyond was even better. A windowless space, it featured eight computers, two printers and numerous maps, tacked to the walls at neat intervals.

"Records of the tides," Aine said, "As well as my habitat maps."

Ravi took a closer look. "This looks like the wormhole."

"'tis."

"We were in there, Tadgh and myself."

"Well done lads, did you see the auks and the wolves?"

Ravi and Tadgh smiled at each other.

"They didn't believe us!" Tadgh practically shouted.

"Their loss isn't it? Pity, they'd have loved them as well."

Freya and Maisie exchanged glances. For the first time, Freya began to seriously consider taking the plunge, literally, into the wormhole.

"I'd like to visit, but I'm not a strong swimmer. I'm totally uncoordinated," Freya said.

"Not to worry, the animals will carry you," Aine replied.

"Really?"

She nodded. "Absolutely. It's considered a place of honor to assist. Come."

The girls walked over to the wall. Aine pointed at a spot on the map of the serpent's lair and the surrounding waters.

"Here's the hospitality suite so to speak. Reception. Where they meet the others, as we're known."

"Hmm I don't know. Is there any other way to get there?"

"No. You must jump in."

Freya bit her lip. "The rocks. How do you keep from knocking your head on them? And how do you hold your breath for so long?"

"Not to worry, you won't hurt yourself. And you don't have to hold your breath for more than a minute." Aine looked at Tadgh and Ravi. "Right, fellas?"

Tadgh nodded. "I'm no good at sport, you've seen me. I've nearly drowned many the time. But I made it down and back. You will too, Freya."

Freya sighed. Although she hated a large part of her life, it was still her life. She'd never been much of a daredevil as she'd seen a boy break both of his legs while trying out a risky skateboard stunt when she was seven. She'd have to think about whether she wanted to take the chance of hurting herself. Or worse.

"I'll think about it."

"Think about it? I thought you were the one all hot for swimming," Quinn said from the door. "Aine, I like your servers."

"Thanks."

"It's like a lair in here," Ravi added. "So many computers."

"I've done a fair bit of ... I know my way around a keyboard."

"Respect," Quinn said.

Aine smiled. "Ah, where have my manners got to? The lot of you must be starved. I don't think they feed you well up at that gaol do they?"

They all exchanged glances.

"How did you know?" Maisie asked.

"This is a tiny island. Any strangers about for more than a speck of time, of your age, surely they're doing time up there. Not to worry though, I was in such a facility myself in my day and I lived to tell. Now how about some scones and clotted cream? And of course a cuppa."

"Thanks," Quinn said.

They followed Aine back into the enormous kitchen, where she put up the kettle. As they waited for the boil, Freya looked back into the room with the computers. A printer hummed to life, spitting out pages of documents in the corner.

"I've been waiting for people such as yourselves for forever. Believers. The ones able to see past convention. Into the serpent's lair."

"Aren't you afraid?" Freya asked.

"What is there to fear? The animals are gentle. They treat me as guests in their home, the way I'm treating you. You're not afraid of me, are you?"

"Of course not."

"Right then, drink up."

After their tea, they had to get back to St. Dymphna's. As they approached, they could see everyone gathered on the spot where announcements were made. The green shirts were standing atop chairs.

"Gather round," Hannah called out, "We've a bit of news."

Freya's chest muscles tightened. "News" was never good, at least in her world. "News" was "your father's left and it's your fault," or "we've no money for Turkish delight," or Freya's favorite, "What do you mean, you want a birthday party? I'm the one who gave my life for you, I'm the one you should be celebrating."

"Rumor has it there's been far too much free time for you lot," Hannah began. "Therefore be advised we'll be instigatin' group projects week after next. You'll be in groups of four, five or six ... what is it down there?"

"Can we choose our groups?"

Hannah turned to Lexie, who nodded.

"Yeah, I suppose so. Less work for us."

The counselors all laughed.

"Your projects will be very important. An assessment will be made. Those of you who rise to the occasion will have your attendance here at St. Dymphna's stricken for forever from our permanent records. Those who fail to meet standards, well, let's just say St. Dymphna's will be with you 'til the end of your days."

"No pressure," Ravi whispered.

For the second time in his life, Quinn was worried his

family would leave him out to dry if he didn't rise up to their expectations. They'd sent him to this reform school in a desolate, dreary part of Ireland without his consent. If they felt he continued to disappoint them, he could wave good-bye to the cushioned life his older brothers and sisters enjoyed.

ELEVEN

They stopped by Aine's place on their next free afternoon, but the ramshackle cottage was shuttered. Even the bees appeared to have gone missing. Perhaps everything was tucked away because there had been rumor of a storm, although it had ultimately blown back over the sea. Quinn took a quick walk around the place, eventually giving them a thumbs down. Everyone was disappointed.

"Right then, on to the wormhole," Ravi said.

Freya took a deep breath. She'd dressed in lightweight clothes in anticipation of the swim she was going to take this afternoon. Maisie had warned her that wet clothing was very heavy and would impede her ability to swim, a fact that frightened Freya almost as much as jumping into the wormhole.

As they approached the rocks, Ravi reached out for her hand. He squeezed her fingers.

"You'll do great, and I'll be right there with you. We're all going down as one."

Freya's mood lifted. Surely she'd be all right as long as she wasn't alone.

"Do you think the animals will be there?"

"I've no idea, but I hope so."

Freya busied herself for the remainder of the climb down to the serpent's lair by thinking about Ravi's drawings.

"Where did you learn to draw like that? Did you take lessons?"

"No! My father's very angry every time he sees me with a pencil in my hand. Says he didn't come to Ireland to see his son fall into 'artistic delusions.' Mum nicks scratch paper from his office, the bits from the copier that are bent, or the till register tapes we're recycling, and she gets pencils from a friend of hers. My little sister watches a lot of telly so I draw whatever I see on the screen. Or at the park. Or in the shop."

"Very cool."

"Thanks."

They'd arrived at the wormhole far too soon for Freya's liking. Her heart beat against her jacket as she stared down into the swirling green, grey and blue water. She was so overcome with fear she was afraid she wouldn't be able to breathe.

"You all right?" Ravi's eyes were wide.

Freya nodded.

"Don't worry, remember. We're all together. Strength in numbers and all that."

"Okay," Freya whispered.

"You'll be grand," Maisie added, offering her hand.

"On three," Ravi said.

"Three, two, one. Go!" Maisie shrieked.

Freya felt her feet leave the ground as they jumped into the swirling waters. Seconds later they were at the serpent's lair. They quickly dropped through the opening, into the entrance to the other world Ravi and Tadgh had visited. A paradise.

It was incredibly light. Sunlight streamed from above the water. Freya opened her mouth. To her amazement, she inhaled the freshest air. She could almost taste the blackberries on the brambles in the distance. The scent of primroses, shamrocks and clover was carried on the gentle wind. Butterflies and birds flew around her, their wings flapping. A pack of elks stood on a slight hill in the distance, their antlers tall and wide. A tiny brown bear appeared at her feet, smiling up at her, its arms outstretched. Freya let go of Maisie and Ravi's hands and dropped to the velvet grass. The bear wrapped its arms around her. Nearby, Tadgh was riding atop a whale, while Quinn was diving into a pool of water with two great auks.

Ravi was sketching it all, capturing every moment, until a corn bunting landed atop his paper. He smiled and watched as it helped guide his pencil. Next to him, Maisie was showing a wildcat how to dance on tiptoe.

Freya let out a whoop of joy. She'd never been so free, or so happy. She had no idea how long they were in the wormhole, and she didn't care. Time had no meaning in this alternate universe.

The light above them shifted. The water in the pools of water began to shake. As if called by an invisible signal, the animals retreated, the grey wolves waving good-bye.

"I don't want to leave." Freya practically sobbed.

Quinn clapped his hands. "Grab onto each other. We have to get out of here. Now, before we miss our window."

Suddenly Freya was afraid. Would they be stuck in here forever? There was no trace of the paradise that had just been, merely empty, dead space.

"Is the water going to fill this space?"

Quinn nodded. "We have time. Just don't look back. As long as we stick together, we'll make it out okay."

They grabbed hands again and jumped up, into the pool of water that had appeared above their heads. Foaming waves pushed them, back and forth, toward the surface. A moment later, they were in the rocky enclosure of the wormhole.

"Grab onto the edge of the rocks," Quinn shouted.

They swam to the limestone jutting into the sea. Tadgh and Quinn pulled themselves up onto the rocks, then reached back for the others. Ravi helped Freya, grasping her elbows, pushing her feet up until she was on the rocks. Then he aided Maisie, who was still carefully guarding her feet. Finally, Tadgh pulled Ravi out of the water. They all laid on the rocks, watching the storm roll in, until the clouds came close enough that they knew they'd drown if they didn't reach higher ground.

"We have to make a pact," Quinn declared as they walked back to St. Dymphna's Holiday Academy. "No one, and I mean no one, can learn about the wormhole. If we were to say we'd been in the serpent's lair, they'd have us locked in isolation for the duration."

"Really?" Tadgh asked. "It's such a great story."

"We'd be declared mad. Isolation would be the least of our troubles," Maisie said. "Trust me, you do not want to be taken for one who lives in a fantasy world. A friend of my brother's was hauled off to a care home for sayin' he'd had visions."

"That settles it," Ravi said, nodding at Tadgh. "This is our secret."

He stuck out his hand. They all piled their hands on top. Secrecy it would be.

The trip to the wormhole was all Freya, Maisie, Quinn, Ravi and Tadgh could think about or discuss. Doing chores, watching the stars at night, eating on the worn wooden tables. It didn't matter where they were, their hearts and minds were beyond the serpent's lair. The extinct animals had become an obsession.

St. Dymphna's was recently endowed by a woman who credited the holiday academy with totally changing the direction of her son's life. Rumor had it he was one of the big tech bosses on the Silicon Docks by the Liffey although no one could ever be sure, since the school was discreet provided its "campers" complied with all directives. The grateful mother decided that the one thing the campers needed was a good library, focused especially on books featuring the Aran Islands, since very few people knew much about the remote area.

Freya, Maisie, Quinn, Ravi and Tadgh took to hurrying through their chores so they could meet in the library and read up on all the Irish animals that had gone extinct. They wanted to know who exactly they were meeting in the wormhole, and what their lives had been like.

"Does it ever make you feel helpless?" Maisie whispered one afternoon as they sat around a table piled high with illustrated books.

Although she'd never admit it to the others, this was the first time in her life she'd felt somewhat brainy. It was lovely to feel she was on top of things, instead of struggling to keep up.

"Like something could have, should have been done," Freya said.

"Exactly."

They looked over at Tadgh, who was trying very hard to stifle a sob.

"Dust to dust," he muttered.

"Truth," Ravi said. "But I agree with Freya. Something has to be done. We can't fix the past, but the future's still out there, waiting to be molded."

Freya smiled.

"Something should have been done. Beyond just hunting bans. Humans have an obligation. Aren't we the ones put on this planet to think?" Maisie shocked herself with her thoughtful comment.

"I'm not so sure about that," Quinn said. "Have you taken a look around lately?"

Ravi rolled his eyes. "Fair play, but you know what Maisie means."

Quinn nodded. "Stewardship is what I call it, what I'm doing with my hives. I'm making sure they thrive. Seeing no harm comes to them as best I can. Preserving, conserving them for the future. So they're not like the Andrena rosae and the Normada sheppardana."

"Let me guess, they are no more." Maisie drew a line across her throat with her finger.

"Sadly yes."

"Well that blows," said Ravi. He sat up straight. "That's it then, it's on us. We're the ones who will make sure it never happens again."

"Easier said than done," Quinn mumbled. "Easier said than done."

TWELVE

Brie was annoyed. None of the campers seemed to be taking all of the challenges presented by the counselors very seriously. They were just coasting, doing the bare minimum of chores, counting down the days until they were dismissed. They just didn't understand how close to the edge far too many of them were standing. Very few were like Tadgh, at the holiday academy for merely social reasons. More of them were like Maisie, in real danger of failing out of school if they didn't develop some measure of self-discipline. Brie sighed. She and Seamus wanted them to succeed. Although they never told the campers, since it would make them seem far too human and take away the fear factor that gave them authority, all of the counselors were former inmates of St. Dymphna's, as the alumni of the holiday academy called themselves. They knew tough love was the only way.

Of all the campers at St. Dymphna's Holiday Academy, Brie, Seamus and Hannah were most worried about Freya and Quinn. Freya was one of the most headstrong campers they'd ever met, and Quinn was a posh boy who'd never lost the maddening, lazy attitude that this whole summer was just for show. He exuded the air that he could, and would, somehow buy his way out of any unpleasant situation. Brie was still disgusted at his smug attitude about his phone, the way he'd told her she'd be replacing it if it was damaged.

The counselors were sitting at the fireplace in their lodge, hands wrapped around mugs of warm tea, fresh from a discussion about Freya and Quinn. Only two weeks remained in the holiday session, and they were frustrated.

"I don't think you pair should deal with them," Lexie said, looking at Brie and Seamus. "You're both far too invested."

Seamus narrowed his eyes. "I'm head here."

"Fair play, but you're not getting the results."

"Lexie."

Hannah's tone was sharp.

Lexie knew she was playing a dangerous game. If Seamus and Brie turned on her, not only would her future at St. Dymphna's be over, so would her career in adolescent counseling. She might as well drop out of Trinity right now. But she couldn't sit by and watch as Seamus and Brie considered sabotaging Freya and Quinn. They were nothing short of obsessed with how much they loathed them. She was pretty sure that their anger toward the pair was largely down to personal dislike. Growing up, Lexie and her sister had cowered in fear as their father raged, often throwing things at their older brother merely because he looked like his dead mother. She had devoted herself to helping people she thought were wrongfully punished. It was the only way to assuage her guilt at not intervening on her brother's behalf.

"Let me supervise all those guys from the back of the bus."

Brie and Seamus looked at each other. They were both accustomed to the adoring gazes of the campers by this stage of the summer. It was true, Maisie, Ravi and Tadgh also didn't share in an affection bordering on adoration for their counselors. Perhaps it would be best if Lexie took the disagreeable campers.

"Okay," Brie finally said.

Although Lexie had no way of knowing this, Freya, Maisie, Quinn, Ravi and Tadgh saw the other campers, especially the ones who openly adored Brie and Seamus, as "victims of Stockholm Syndrome." It had been Maisie who had first suggested the other campers had fallen prey to "siding with our captors" as she put it, although Tadgh thought calling the counselors jailers was rather harsh.

They were sitting on a stone slab, waiting to hear how long their free time would last this afternoon. One free hour would allow a quick visit to Aine. More than two hours and they'd have time to head for the wormhole. They were placing bets on which it was to be as Lexie approached. Quinn groaned when he noticed her coming their way. Lexie pretended not to hear. She could hardly blame him; surely they were all aware of how much they were hated by Brie and Seamus. Lexie forced herself to smile.

"My favorite members of this summer's crop," she said, far too brightly.

Freya rolled her eyes. She knew they were being had. Everyone recognized being played.

"What do you want?" Maisie forced herself to be pleasant. "We have finished our chores, we're just waiting, along with the others."

Lexie heard the defensiveness in Maisie's tone.

"Not to worry, I'm here to say you're going to crush the others at the competition."

Tadgh sat up straighter and smiled.

Lexie still hadn't quite figured out what was wrong with him, but it didn't matter. As far as she was concerned, Tadgh was the camper who had made the most progress this year.

He'd come into himself and made friends. She smiled at him before she turned to the whole group.

"I'm not supposed to be helping...."

Freya narrowed her eyes. Surely this was a trick?

"I think you five have it in you to win the big prize."

"Which is what?" Ravi leaned forward.

"The group who creates the best project, shows the most teamwork, will be allowed totally free reign the last two days of the holiday academy. You'll be able to explore Inis Mor at your leisure."

They looked at each other. Two days of swimming with the animals, visiting Aine and sunning themselves at the entrance to the serpent's lair.

"How do we win?"

Lexie smiled to herself. She wasn't surprised Quinn would want to triumph. Those posh campers always returned to their natural habits.

"Create something irresistible. You need to come up with a project that will leave everyone drooling. Wondering how you did it."

"What kinds of projects won in past years?" Maisie asked.

Lexie shook her head. "We're not kidding when we say everything that happens here remains in confidence. Sealed. Inaccessible to others."

"So you can't tell us," Ravi said.

"I'm afraid not." Lexie brushed her hair from her eyes. "All I can say is I've faith in you."

"Thanks," Tadgh said.

They watched her walk away.

"We have to win. Two free days...."

"We will win."

"How?"

They watched the others gathering in small groups.

"What do you think they're all doing?"

"Plotting ways to suck up to the counselors."

"No, I mean what do you think their projects are?" Maisie asked.

"Who cares?" Ravi shrugged. "We have to think about our project."

"We need something really big," Freya said. "My granny always used to say the best way to make others feel important is to make them feel like they're part of something big."

"Like my dance squad," Maisie said. "We're all there for each other. One big wig with a lot of little curls."

"A club," Quinn said slowly.

Freya rolled her eyes. Of course the posh kid would suggest a club.

"A conservation club."

"I like it," Ravi said.

"We save the animals," Tadgh said.

"Yes!" Maisie raised her fist in the air.

"Not bad," Freya admitted.

"What's our name to be? Very important, the name."

"The Misfits Club." Tadgh was very certain.

Quinn scowled. He hadn't said anything when Tadgh had labelled them the misfits on the bus ride to St. Dymphna's. But that was because it was only a term used among themselves. He'd always been one of the cool kids. He was not okay with being labelled a loser when he was the opposite of a misfit. He glanced over at Maisie. She was also frowning. Clearly they were of the same mind.

On the other hand, maybe Tadgh was right. They were here, at a glorified reform school, because they didn't fit in with social norms. And Quinn was sick of hearing how he didn't live up to his parents' social expectations. Even his eldest brother, Gavin, had begun to ride him about his lack of performance. Wouldn't they be horrified if he branded himself a misfit? The thought of Glynnis and Oliver's faces, their feeble attempts to justify such a self-imposed description to their friends, well, it could be a lot of fun to watch. Payback for sending him away for the summer. The fact he'd enjoyed himself still didn't take away the sting of their betrayal.

"I'm in. Maisie?"

She looked at Quinn.

He smiled and nodded.

Maisie smiled back and said, "Count me in."

"Me too," Ravi said,

"Brilliant name," Freya added, although she thought it was ridiculous.

Shouldn't a conservation club for animals say something about nature? She shrugged. She knew it didn't matter. After all, Lexie had been adamant that whatever happened at St. Dymphna's Holiday Academy remained on Inis Mor. And with no mobile phones, there was no record of anything. No harm in claiming the misfit label. It would never go beyond the Aran Islands.

"What exactly will our club do?" Maisie asked.

"We'll save the animals," Tadgh repeated.

His eyes were wide and shiny. "We make a plan. People our age, all over the world, they clean up the beaches and the parks and they make sure no trash hits the water. No trash in the water, no trash in the forest, no trash in nature."

"I'm not sure that's very unique," Maisie said. "Just sounds like picking up after yourself."

Freya sighed. The idea was not bad, but there was nothing unique about it. Practically every school in Ireland already had a conservation group. There had to be something more if they were to win the competition. "What if we say the club is for us, the kids? That it's a place where everyone belongs. The only requirement is no slagging on others."

"And no grown-ups. Ever," Maisie added. "They take over everything."

"Now that's an idea." Ravi gave a thumbs up.

And so The Misfits Club was born.

"If we're going to win the three days off we have to take this seriously," Quinn said.

"Agreed," Freya replied.

The other three nodded.

Everyone helped. Ravi made a logo with grey wolves swimming with great auks as a flock of corn bunting hover. Maisie drafted a code of conduct similar to the ones she was used to seeing for the feis. Freya and Quinn created a manifesto. The Misfits Club would honor all creatures, living and extinct.

"We need a mission statement," Quinn said. "All the companies my da represents have them."

"What's that?" Ravi asked.

"A clear statement about our goals."

"Save the world!" Tadgh called out. "We are the superheros!"

They all smiled.

"Pretty cool."

"Yeah."

"The animals," Freya said.

"Don't be an eejit," Quinn replied. "Our overriding goal is an animal sanctuary."

"How are we going to do that?"

"Easy. Once the parks and beaches are cleaned and cleared, the animals will come back and claim their places. Each Misfits Club will choose an area they want to preserve. They'll clean up with the goal of making the space hospitable for the animals. Like my bees. I have to tend the hives, give the bees what they need or they'll die."

"So the clubs all have different animals they're saving, based on which animals live nearby." Maisie's voice shook with excitement. "How cool is that!"

"We'll bring back the dead animals," Tadgh said.

"I'm not sure how that'll work."

Tadgh looked at them in disbelief. "How can you say that? You saw them with your eyes."

Freya gently laid her hand on his arm. "They're in the wormhole."

"We can bring them back."

Tadgh sounded like the twins when they needed a nap.

"That's very good idea, Tadgh."

They exchanged looks once more. Just when they thought Tadgh was like them, he said something a bit off.

Lexie sounded the gong that called them all to dinner. Freya was glad for the distraction. Sometimes she worried about Tadgh.

THIRTEEN

The next afternoon, they had an hour of free time. While the other groups worked on their projects, Freya, Maisie, Quinn, Ravi and Tadgh snuck off for a visit to Aine. As they approached her cottage, they heard music. Strings and faint drums. They could never quite tell where the music came from, it just seemed to surround Aine.

"The bees are loose!" Maisie shrieked. She pointed to Freya.

Yellow and black insects had surrounded around Freya. She stood completely still, her hands over her eyes and mouth. Terrified, she feared the bees would swarm into her ears. Or perhaps make their way through her fingers. After a moment, her knees began to tremble.

Quinn stepped forward, peering at the insects. "It's okay, Freya, they're not bees."

"Wasps!" Tadgh cried.

"No, no no, they're just hornet moths. Don't worry, Freya, they won't hurt you."

"Sure about that?"

"Yep."

Freya carefully peered out between her fingers. Several of

the hornet moths were still flying in a circle in front of her. She squeezed her eyes closed.

"They're vegetarian," Quinn said loudly. "They've zero interest in hurting humans."

"Really?"

"Yeah. They're vegetarian and extinct."

"What?" Ravi's eyes widened.

"Very cool." Tadgh smiled.

Freya finally calmed down enough to remove her hands from her face. She was exhausted from the fear. But she knew Quinn was an expert on bees. If he said she could relax, things would be fine. She looked at the bright insects. Their colors were stunning.

None of them were surprised a crew of extinct insects had set up at Aine's place. It was very cozy, and everything about her and the cottage exuded warmth and safety. No wonder the hives were so happy. Quinn went to check on them as Aine appeared from behind the cottage, carrying an armful of wild-flowers.

"Welcome! So lovely to see you today. Come in, or would you rather sit on the terrace? It's a fine day."

"The terrace please." Maisie plopped down on the fat cushion atop the love seat. Freya slid into place on her left.

"I'll fetch some biscuits and tea. And we're in luck, I've a pan of scones just out the oven."

Freya leaned against the pillow. She was going to miss Aine, and this place. It was a true refuge.

"What's it to be, green tea or one of the smarter flavors?"

"Whatever you have on hand," Maisie said, glancing at the others. "We don't want to be a bother."

"Nonsense, I adore your visits. Lovely to finally meet others who care so much about the animals. Back in a mo."

They relaxed as Quinn studied the bees. He was so

intrigued at the patterns of the hives. They were unlike his bees, or his grandfather's, although he wasn't quite sure why. They seemed almost fossilized, although of course that was ridiculous, as they were buzzing around.

"There we are, and cream and brown sugar for Tadgh."

He smiled at Aine. It was refreshing to be remembered.

"An afternoon at your leisure again? Good to see they're cutting you some slack."

"We've only nine more days," Maisie said. "I think they dial it down at the end."

"Only for us," Freya reminded everyone, "As we've finished our project."

"And what might that be?"

"We're starting a club to create pocket animal sanctuaries. It was Tadgh's idea."

He blushed. "Ah, listen to you, it was all of us."

"Credit where it's due," Ravi said. "This was mainly your plan."

"The Misfits Club," Tadgh said proudly. "I chose the name."

"Isn't that perfect?" Aine sipped her tea. "It works on so many levels."

They all sat in silence.

Finally, Maisie said, "Am I the only one who doesn't understand?"

"What's that, Maisie?" Aine cocked her head like a puzzled dog.

"The levels?"

"Ah, right. Well, St. Dymphna's Holiday Academy is for those judged to be a bit misfit. As all geniuses and creatives are. The unconventional are never recognized in their time. You all know that, right? You are the chosen. Oh it's hard to see it now, what with studies and parents and the slagging and the snark that goes with adolescence. You're the special ones. The stand outs."

"Sometimes it doesn't feel that way."

Aine nodded. "Of course not, Freya. But you'll see. One of these days you'll realize your genius."

They all smiled.

"It's beyond you lot, though. Misfits, again, the 'misfits.' An apt description for our endangered animals. Like you, they're struggling because they don't fit into their environments either. They began perfectly suited to their habitats, but then conditions changed."

"That's what we want to stop," Ravi said, "Conditions changing."

"A laudable goal." Aine set down her cup and picked up the tea pot. "Top anyone off?"

Tadgh watched the hornet moths fluttering in the distance. He leaned forward. "You have to help the animals. Bring them back to life."

Freya's back tightened. Tadgh and his obsession with the extinct animals made her more than a little uncomfortable. It seemed he was refusing to accept reality, something Mam had always struggled with. Freya knew that denial brought about nothing but pain.

Aine patted Tadgh's knee. "I'm afraid you overestimate me, Tadgh."

"No, I saw. The moths." He looked back in their direction, but they had disappeared. "And your potions. I saw all the jars, on the hob, on the bureau. Magic potions."

"The only magic in those jars is of the cosmetic kind."

"You have to help us bring the extinct animals back. Please."

"Oh Tadgh, you suffer for nothing. The animals aren't extinct."

Tadgh puffed out his chest. "I most certainly did see them, with my own eyes. Beyond the serpent's lair. I swam with the whales. Rode on the backs of the brown bears. I patted a grey wolf."

"Of course you did, love. You all did." Aine smiled.

"The extinct animals," Tadgh repeated. "I saw them, on your charts and maps."

Aine shook her head. "I never use that word. The animals are not extinct. They've merely moved on. As you said, you all saw them with your own eyes. The animals are in their own world. A parallel universe to be sure, but they're grand."

Tadgh put his head in his hands. Aine rubbed his back as if he were an infant. "There, there, it's all right. The animals have found a new world where they fit."

He didn't say anything for the rest of the visit. Tadgh just trailed Quinn as he looked at the bees, listened to the sound of Maisie's feet as she danced on the stone terrace and watched Freya and Ravi study the maps of the tides, their heads bent close. When it was time to leave, Aine gave them each a hug.

The air was cool and crisp, slightly stinging their faces as they walked back to St. Dymphna's.

"I'm sorry about the animals," Ravi said. "I know you wanted to bring them back. But like Aine said, they're not gone. They've just moved."

Tadgh nodded.

"It's still rough," Freya said quietly. "I understand."

Tadgh wiped a tear from his eye.

Freya suddenly realized that Tadgh would likely always be a misfit. While the others would go on to lead their lives, he would always be in the shadows. St. Dymphna's might very well be the only time in his life when he had friends. Belonged. She turned away to hide her sadness.

FOURTEEN

Brie shook the bell she loved to use to summon the campers. She felt it gave St. Dymphna's a homey touch, since her gran used a bell to call them to tea on her farm in the northwest. The campers emerged from all corners of the St. Dymphna's Holiday Academy. Brie was constantly amazed at the odd places some of the "guests" chose to visit. There were campers who actually enjoyed hanging out behind the cabins, where it smelled of mold. Campers who liked sitting beneath trees that had bugs crawling across their roots. Those who reveled in lying in the mud.

But the oddest of all were the campers who never left the cabins. Every session there were a handful of boys and girls who spent all their free time on their bunks. As a nature lover, Brie was dumbfounded that anyone would choose to stay indoors when there was so much to explore on Inis Mor. Every year she was surprised that the special projects never seemed to give even a passing nod to the unique setting of St. Dymphna's. It was discouraging.

Slowly the campers staggered out to the main sitting area. Brie frowned when she spotted Freya, Maisie, Quinn, Ravi and

Tadgh. Those five had made no effort whatsoever to interact with any of the others. She was certain they'd been strangers when they boarded the bus in Dublin, though by the time they'd reach the holiday academy them seemed to be the best of friends. If she was honest with herself, Brie was a bit jealous of their close bond. She'd tried so hard to forge ties with Hannah and Lexie, but they never seemed interested. Only Seamus was remotely friendly, and she suspected that was because, like her, he was a huge fan of following the rules.

Seamus, Hannah and Lexie were already seated at the table they'd dragged out from their lounge, ready to address the campers. This was a very important day. The counselors would announce the winners of the competition. Every year there had been fights among the counselors about who should win. That had led Seamus to declare the need for anonymous judging. The projects could stand on their own. The needs of the campers would not be considered, nor would their relationships to the counselors. Brie had been rather sour when Seamus had made this decision, for she believed an important part of the St. Dymphna's Holiday Academy was learning to respect authority. But Lexie had won her over with the claim that the most important thing all the campers were doing was learning to respect themselves.

"It's a big day, as you well know," Brie bellowed through her megaphone. "The selection of the winners of this year's prize for the best holiday academy project. As you may remember, the winning team will have two free days to explore Inis Mor before our session ends."

"As if we need reminded." Maisie rolled her eyes.

They were sitting at the far edge of the group, half turned away. Brie noticed their apathy. She narrowed her eyes. Although she prided herself on not being petty, she had a measure of joy knowing this group would never win the prize.

They'd certainly been the ones who handed in the late project, which was an automatic disqualification. Every year, one group refused to follow the rules. She sighed, then looked at Seamus, who nodded.

"Third prize goes to the group who created the mop drop project, a unique way to clean a dirty cabin floor."

There was polite applause.

"We made it through that round," Tadgh whispered.

Freya smiled at him.

"Next, our runner up, in second place, is the group who created 'The New Rules Handbook' for incoming campers."

Brie took a deep breath. At first this had been her favorite project. But when the final project was submitted, she had to agree with Seamus, Hannah and Lexie. Unlike in many years past, there was one clear winner. One project that embodied the spirit of true rebirth.

"And finally, we come to our winner. For the first time in the history of St. Dymphna's Holiday Academy, the judges have a unanimous verdict. In first place is 'The Misfits Club.'"

Tadgh clapped wildly.

"The Misfits Club is an environmental group whose mission is to save endangered animals by cleaning up their habitats. Club members will meet in parks, on beaches, anywhere in need of a deep clean. The only rule? No grown-ups."

Everyone cheered.

"The Misfits Club was created by," Brie opened an envelope, "Freya, Maisie, Quinn, Ravi and Tadgh."

Brie bit her lip to keep herself from expressing her surprise.

"Congratulations!" Lexie yelled.

The Misfits stood and hugged each other. A minute later they were surrounded by other campers. High fives and hugs were exchanged.

"We did it!" Maisie squealed.

Freya glanced over at Quinn. He didn't seem the least bit surprised. Once again she was reminded of how different she was from the rest of them. Even if he was at St. Dymphna's, he was used to winning. The same thing with Maisie. And Ravi and Tadgh were also surrounded by people who would give hugs and high fives when they returned to Dublin. Although she was happy they'd won, a heavy sadness settled in her chest. Only a few more days and she'd return to life alone.

"You all right?" Ravi's eyes were wide.

"Sure, I'm just thinking about how great it is we won."

Ravi nodded. "More time at the wormhole."

"I can't wait."

"Tomorrow morning," Tadgh said.

"For sure." Maisie smiled.

The girls in Freya's cabin were surprisingly nice.

"Pretty cool you won," Siobhan said as they were putting out the lights.

"Thanks."

For the first time all summer, Freya fell into a deep sleep the minute she pulled up the rough wool blanket. The rain pelting the rooftop reminded her of the waterfall she'd glimpsed in the wormhole. She could hardly wait to return.

But the next morning, the rains were so heavy it was like a curtain of water had been hung from the clouds. It was almost impossible to see more than a few feet ahead, let alone find their way to the serpent's lair. Freya waded to the dining hall, biting her lip to keep from crying in disappointment. Ravi and Tadgh were nursing cups of tea, huddled against the wind that kept blowing the door open.

"Maybe it'll blow over," Ravi said.

"More likely blow us over," Tadgh said.

"Is there any way?"

Ravi shook his head. "Too dangerous, Freya, we'd slip on the rocks."

Freya sighed. Slipping on the rocks was something she and Maisie feared. Sadly, if it rained hard all day, there was no way the rocks would be dry tomorrow.

"We won for nothing."

"Not true."

Quinn sat down in the empty seat across from Tadgh. "We'll get our trip to the wormhole in, I'm sure of it."

"The resident optimist," Ravi said.

Quinn didn't laugh.

Maisie joined them a few minutes later. They spent the morning playing card games, trying to distract themselves with endless cups of tea. Finally, when they could stand it no more, the rain let up a bit.

"The ruins," Quinn said. "We'll hit the ruins. There's loads to see here, we might as well make a day of it."

"Fair enough."

They grabbed their rain gear and headed out.

"Mind the grikes," Quinn called out as they came across a particularly slippery collection of crisscrossed limestone rocks.

"I'd better not wreck my feet. I've spent all summer guarding them."

"You'll be fine, Maisie," Tadgh said.

Freya glanced at Maisie's feet, still inside her best trainers. There was no way the trainers would ever fit properly as Maisie's feet were clearly bigger. She dreaded what Mam would have to say about her loaning out her shoes. More than likely she'd not be allowed a replacement pair.

They climbed a slight hill and came upon stone graves marked with Celtic crosses. Several people wearing backpacks were hiking nearby, carrying carrier bags Freya was sure contained take-away lunches.

"Maybe we can stop by Aine's for tea."

"Depends on the weather," Quinn shouted over the wind.

Luckily, the storm blew out to sea. The ground was still slick and the air misty, but they could handle a soft day.

"Let's see the forts. It's the one thing Inis Mor is famous for. Besides the wormhole," Ravi said.

"I'm on it." Quinn looked around, getting his bearings.

A moment later they were headed to Dun Duchathair, the black fort that stretched out into the sea.

"*Clochan*," Quinn announced as they stood in front of some stone ruins. "An old beehive hut."

"Very cool," Ravi said.

It stopped raining. A weak sun streaked the sky.

"Now on to Aine!" Freya and Maisie shouted in unison.

"Any idea where her place is from here, Quinn?"

Quinn studied the horizon. Ravi was right, he was like a human compass. After a few minutes, he had them walking in the direction of Aine's cottage. He couldn't wait to talk to her about the *clochan*. Surely she must have visited in the past.

She was in the garden, tending one of the hives, when they arrived.

"We've been expecting you." She nodded toward the bees. "Time for a cuppa and a chat."

Aine led them in to sit before the turf fire in her lounge. "I assume you won the competition."

"How'd you know?" Ravi asked.

"Like I said, you're the visionaries. Don't you forget it. You'll be far from this island soon, but the island will never be far from you."

She looked at Freya and smiled.

Freya had never felt so understood by an adult before.

"Tell me about the *clochan*."

"How did you know?" Tadgh could hardly believe it.

Aine smiled. "We are on the same, eternal wavelength."

She pointed at her head, then her heart.

For the next five minutes, Quinn and Aine had a detailed discussion about all the bees that had disappeared from Ireland, the ones who were endangered and the plentiful types who buzzed around Dublin. Aine called them city bees and joked that they carried book bags and wore eyeglasses.

"Tell me, have you seen the seals?" Aine asked.

They shook their heads.

Aine stood. "You can't leave Inis Mor without a visit to their colony. It's low tide. The perfect time for a visit."

They trekked to the beach that held the seal colony. A dozen enormous grey seals were sunning themselves on the rocks, their faces turned to the sky.

"They're not … endangered?" Tadgh could barely say the word.

"Not to worry, Tadgh, we've plenty. See for yourself." Aine pointed out to sea.

Seals were frolicking in the surf.

"It's a fine, fragile world we live in," Aine said. "We're all interconnected. Lucky are we to have known each other."

They all smiled.

A few minutes later, Aine headed back to her cottage and Freya, Maisie, Quinn, Ravi and Tadgh began the hike back to St. Dymphna's, all of them sad their time together was coming to an end.

FIFTEEN

"Freya. Freya!"

Freya pulled the blanket over her head. "Off me, Nora, I'll be up in a mo."

"Freya!"

She sighed. Allie must be with Nora. She'd no idea the pair of them were so strong.

"Get up! Now! It's our last day!"

Someone – Allie? Nora? Mam? – pulled back the cover.

Freya rubbed her eyes. Maisie was standing over her, frowning.

"Time to visit the wormhole!"

Freya sat up. She couldn't believe it, oversleeping on the day she'd most anticipated. Whenever she was under stress, Freya escaped into a dream world. After Da left, Mam said it had been like waking the dead to get her up for school. She never imagined she'd have failed to wake up on such an exciting morning. Maisie was standing next to her bunk. Otherwise the cabin was empty.

"What time is it? Where are the others?"

Maisie shrugged. "I don't know. Doing chores. Cementing their status as members of the Stockholm Syndrome Club."

Freya didn't laugh.

"Come on, it's okay. No one else is ready for the wormhole."

Of course the minute they got outside, Freya realized they'd all been waiting for her, although no one was rude enough to say so. Ravi had laid many more illustrations on the drawing she'd seen him working on yesterday and Tadgh was fidgeting.

"Onward," Quinn said.

"I can't believe it's our last trip to the wormhole," Maisie said as they hiked along the path that led down to the serpent's lair.

"For now," Tadgh said.

Freya glanced at his face. His jaw was tight. Clearly he was also not looking forward to returning home. They hadn't talked about it, and Freya didn't want to ask. She hoped they'd somehow be able to get together, since they all lived in County Dublin.

There was an old man with a walking stick hovering near the rocks when they arrived at Poll na bPeist, which they'd learned was the Irish name for the wormhole. They looked at each other and frowned.

"Now what?" Maisie wailed. "If he sees us going into the serpent's lair he may call the garda. Or try to stop us."

"We wait him out," Tadgh said. "No worries, he'll be gone soon."

"We could scare him away," Quinn said ten minutes later.

"Quinn!"

"Just a thought. Not saying we should do it, at least not yet."

They waited a few more minutes. Tadgh picked up a few stray rocks and pitched them down toward the sea.

"Heads down!"

They could barely stop themselves laughing. They fell into a pile, hiding from view, behind a large rock. When they looked down again, the man was gone.

"Let's go before anyone else decides to show."

They clambered down to the wormhole. Maisie was still guarding her feet – it wouldn't do to wreck them the week she was going back into the dance studio – but even she was quick. Quinn stood in the middle. Freya and Maisie each took one of his hands. Ravi clasped onto Freya's other hand, and Maisie reached for Tadgh.

"See you on the other side!" Quinn yelled as they jumped.

The trip through the serpent's lair, on to the other world, took only a minute. The sun was even brighter than the last time they'd visited, chunks of golden light breaking through the water. As had happened during the last visit to the wormhole, their clothing had miraculously dried when they landed in the other world.

A trio of brown cubs was waiting for Freya. They ran toward her, paws outstretched. She knelt down and let them smother her in hugs. Quinn was immediately surrounded by two species of bees he'd only read about in books. They led him toward their nearby hive.

A small whale popped up from the surf of the nearby sea, nodding at Tadgh. He swam into the water and climbed on its back. Ravi pulled out the tiny pencil and notebook he kept in his back pocket and started sketching all the new flowers and trees. There were many different species than last time. He'd get them down on paper and look them up later.

A group of boars lounged beneath a flowering tree. Birds sang in chorus as a dozen auks marched along the edge of the water. Maisie could feel the beat of their feet reverberating across the rocks. Two grey wolves sidled up next to her, nuzzling her palm. She smiled at them, then began dancing. Maisie closed her eyes, spinning round and round, pretending she was on stage at The Gaiety. To her surprise, when she opened her eyes, the wolves were mimicking her steps. She brushed her feet against the rocks, following with a shuffle. They brushed, then shuffled, their paws.

"Right then, a dancing lesson it is."

For the next half hour, Maisie and the wolves danced. Eventually several other animals joined them. When they were done Quinn and Ravi clapped.

"Brilliant," Quinn said when she joined him on a nearby rock.

A dozen bees flew above his head, high enough that Maisie was not afraid.

"Thanks."

"The maths, you know them all."

"Maths?"

"Sure, it's like football, you've got the vision of where your feet need to land, you're counting the steps, calculating the distance."

"I've never thought of it that way."

"You should."

Ravi sat next to them. He held up his drawings. One of the sketches was Maisie and the wolves. Another was Quinn and the bees. A third drawing showed Tadgh riding the whale as if it was a horse. It reminded Maisie of the wild horses they'd seen on the island. She loved the way their manes blew back with the wind.

"Freya," Maisie said.

Ravi turned the page to a drawing of Freya, surrounded by bear cubs. Which she was, sitting with two of them in her lap, cuddling them as if they were Nora and Allie. She looked over at them and waved. Luckily they were too far away to see the tears in her eyes.

Tadgh was still riding his whale. They came close and Tadgh beckoned. "There's one for each of us. Come on!"

Ravi jumped up and down to catch Freya's attention as Maisie and Quinn went to claim their whales. A moment later they were all atop the grey mammals, riding into another new world of exotic birds, flowering trees and waterfalls. On and on they rode, as if circling the inside of the earth.

"I love the whales!" Quinn shouted.

The sun shone brighter and the water overhead rippled, like a sheer curtain blowing in the wind. Freya wondered would they ride forever? Would the whales ever tire? Just as she was beginning to crave tea, the whales swam into a shallow spot. They lowered themselves into the water so Freya, Maisie, Quinn, Ravi and Tadgh could slide off their backs, onto the outcropping of rocks that stretched into the sea.

"Where are we?" Freya asked.

"How will we get back?" Tadgh's voice shook. "We're on the underside of the world."

"No, just another part of the wormhole."

Ravi bit his lip. "Doesn't that mean we'll re-enter the atmosphere in a different place, maybe even a different time?"

"What? You mean we could be sitting at the round table? In a time before crisps were invented?" Maisie shuddered.

"I don't know," Quinn admitted. "I didn't think this through."

Everyone tried to hide their fear.

"No good," Tadgh said. "We can't worry. We have to try to go back."

Maisie looked at the water. The whales had disappeared. It was obviously very deep.

"I don't see how we'll get back. We can't jump in there, we'll drown."

"Look!" Freya pointed to the elks standing nearby.

"Those antlers."

The elk approached. Their antlers were as wide as wings.

"Let's ride them," Ravi said.

"I don't think they'll like that," Maisie said.

"Watch."

A moment later Ravi sat atop one of the elegant elks. Freya, Maisie, Quinn and Tadgh also mounted the great deer, who carried them back across the new world, through fields of wildflowers and animals grazing, many nodding as they passed. Finally, they arrived back at the serpent's lair.

"Good-bye," Maisie said. "I'm going to miss this world."

"It's not going away," Tadgh said firmly.

"For us it is," Maisie said sadly.

Tadgh took her hand, then reached for Freya. Quinn and Ravi grasped their hands and they stepped into the water, swimming up until they arrived at the rocks. For the last time, Quinn made sure everyone was on the rocks, away from the slippery edge of the wormhole, before he climbed up onto the sturdy ground.

They sat side by side, staring out at the sea, occasionally shivering in their wet clothes. The watched the waves crash and the water slosh onto the rocks. It filled the crevices of the stone slabs, forcing them to climb higher, until finally they were on the path that led back to St. Dymphna's.

Freya always believed that the worst thing about her father leaving was his failure to say good-bye. She woke up early one morning, rushing to the breakfast table, ready for him to pour her cereal in the little bowl with her name painted across the base when they'd been on holiday, but the kitchen was empty. She'd run up the worn steps, her stocking feet slipping on the wooden stairs, panicked something terrible had happened. Screaming "Da, da," she'd run through the flat. But her father was gone. Da had just slipped away, like a piece of paper carried on the breeze. Freya had been so sad, and so scared. For months she'd been afraid to close her eyes, afraid Mam would disappear as well.

Over the past week, whenever Freya thought about leaving Maisie, Ravi, Quinn and Tadgh, she'd begun to think that not saying a proper good-bye might not be so bad. If one never said good-bye, then one wasn't really leaving. Freya couldn't stand the thought of returning to her dreary life with her twin sisters and her drunken mum and the nuns who hated her so much they'd had her exiled to the other end of Ireland. She'd been so happy these past two months. No, Freya told herself, she was merely stepping out of this life for a short time. She needed to kid herself, enjoy the last few precious hours before they boarded the ferry to the mainland and the bus to Dublin tomorrow. Tonight Freya would pretend this new life would stretch forever. They'd sit under the stars and talk about the animals and chew the biscuits Quinn was so adept at sneaking from the counselors' supply when they weren't looking.

The signs were tethered to the cabins.

GOOD-BYE AND GOOD LUCK!

WE BELIEVE IN YOU!

YOU MADE IT – CONGRATULATIONS!

"They've given us a send-off!" Ravi exclaimed.

"Grand!"

"Shocking," Quinn said, although he was smiling.

Several other campers, including two girls who'd been terrible to Freya since the first day, approached them as they walked toward the main gathering spot. They actually waved hello, which made Freya incredibly angry. Why had they waited until the last day to acknowledge her? Her anger quickly mounted when she saw Ravi return the wave.

"We've games and a night of fun!" Hannah called brightly.

Freya bit back her tears. The day had started off late, and now it was ending early. The final evening with just Maisie, Quinn, Ravi and Tadgh she'd anticipated was clearly not going to happen. She took a step back as her friends were surrounded by the other "campers." No one seemed to notice she was missing. It was the story of her life. She'd been so hopeful these past two months, enjoying the sense of belonging. She should have known better.

SIXTEEN

It was Tadgh who noticed Freya leaning against a limestone slab while the others gorged on all the treats and sweets they'd been deprived of for the past two months. He grabbed a cone of blue candy floss and offered it to her as the others danced to the music now blasting from Seamus's phone.

"Thanks."

He leaned against the slab next to Freya. "We did it. Made it through St. Dymphna's Holiday Academy."

"For what that's worth." Freya picked at the candy floss. She loved the way it left dabs of sugar on her tongue.

They stood in silence for a few more minutes, until Quinn sidled up next to them.

"Come on Tadgh, we know you've the moves."

Tadgh was delighted to be asked to join the dancing. Freya followed them to the makeshift dance floor. Tadgh was surprisingly light on his feet. Maisie grabbed his hands and the two of them were eventually the center of the campers. Everyone was smiling, especially Brie.

"Freya, come on girlfriend!"

Freya was pulled into the dancing crowd by Maisie. Soon

she was surrounded by Quinn and Ravi. Tadgh, who was spinning around with other campers, eventually came back to the group. They danced together, beneath the stars, until the music stopped.

"Not to be a kill joy, but the hike to the ferry is early tomorrow, so back to your cabins. Now!" Brie called.

Maisie looked at her friends wistfully. "I can't believe this is it."

She held out her hand. The others put their hands on top of hers.

"Misfits forever!" Tadgh said.

"Misfits forever," Ravi echoed.

"Come on you lot, time to gather your gear. We need all bags packed tonight." Brie pointed at the cabins.

Reluctantly they said good-night.

Freya spent the night fitfully dozing, while Quinn, Ravi and Tadgh talked about the video games they'd missed. Maisie dreamed of dancing with the animals in the wormhole. The next morning, Freya was the first at the meeting spot. She didn't want to miss a minute with her friends. But already she could feel the shift. Everyone's attention was scattered, focused outward as they fell in line for the hike to the ferry that would carry them to the mainland.

"A shame we've no view of the wormhole," Maisie said as they walked.

Freya was swiveling her head about, trying to take pictures in her mind. It would be a long time until she traveled this far again, or saw the sea beyond County Dublin.

Quinn, Ravi and Tadgh moved farther ahead.

"Wait up lads, tryin' to ditch us are you?" Maisie called out.

Quinn looked back over his shoulder. "Ah no."

They all walked on together.

"I'm going to miss Aine," Tadgh said. "Great scones."

"A true one-off," Quinn said.

"Wonder if she's ever lonely," Freya mused. "She'd no photos of any people."

"I don't think she cares about anything but animals and nature," Ravi replied. "She reminded me of those witches my mam has always been afraid of."

"What witches?" Quinn asked.

"The ones she thought roamed the Irish countryside." Ravi shook his head. "She was very into all this superstition about the Celtic goddesses."

"That's cool," Maisie said.

"Fantasies," Ravi said.

"Probably, although who knows? People will think we've gone mad if we tell them what we found at the wormhole," Maisie said.

"Best keep it to ourselves," Tadgh said. "I don't need any more thinkin' I'm not with it."

There was an awkward pause.

"That's absurd," Freya said. "You're the height of cool. Look at the way you dance."

Tadgh beamed.

"Seriously, I don't think we should tell anyone about the animals," Maisie continued.

"Agreed," Quinn said. "Their lives would be in danger if anyone found out."

Ravi laughed. "You can't be serious, man, in danger? They're extinct! They're way past the point of danger."

Freya held her breath. Was this it, the group coming apart, fraying at the center?

Quinn laughed.

Freya exhaled.

The trek to the ferry was over far too soon. Freya was sad to reach the dock, although the others seemed relieved.

"Home," Maisie muttered as they took their places by the rail.

They watched Inis Mor recede into the background. Ironically the crossing was very smooth, as though the water had a truce with the normally choppy wind. The sun shone so brightly Maisie was certain they'd have a burn.

The bus was already waiting for them when they arrived on the mainland. Freya held her breath as the other campers boarded, afraid their seats together would be taken by another group. Quinn pushed his way to the front. When they finally mounted the stairs, Freya could see he'd spread his gear across the back row.

Seamus and Brie accompanied them, along with Lexie, who passed out sweets as soon as they'd ridden past the colorful pubs and window boxes of Galway. The counselors seemed determined to continue the party from last night.

"May we have your attention," Seamus called out. "Eyes and ears here please."

"Rather dramatic," Maisie mumbled.

Freya giggled.

"We congratulate you once more on surviving St. Dymphna's Holiday Academy and welcome you into the band of inmates."

"What?"

"Who are they talking about? Inmates?"

Everyone on the coach was puzzled.

"Welcome to our crew!" Brie shouted. She looked up and down the aisles and smiled. "That's right, we're with you! We have all served our sentences at St. Dymphna's. Our days at the holiday academy changed our lives. As it will for you lot."

"They were at St. Dymphna's?"

"Who knew?"

"We want you to know that wherever you go, we go with you. The spirit of St. Dymphna's will live on in all of you for forever."

Everyone clapped.

"So cool they kept it a secret," Ravi said.

"Yeah, they rock," Quinn added.

Freya was enraged. She'd had it with lies, people hiding who they really were. "You don't think it was a bit nasty to keep it on the down low?"

"No way," Maisie said. "They had to push us. Like my best dance teachers."

"And coaches," Quinn said.

Freya sat back against the rigid seat. She wished she had a teacher or a coach to give life lessons, instead of having to learn everything herself.

Maisie began lightly beating out a beat on the floor. Freya had a sense of déjà vu.

"Wait!" Maisie looked down at her feet. "Your trainers."

She pulled them off her feet, tucked the laces inside and handed them to Freya. "You saved my life."

The trainers were clearly stretched out by Maisie's wide feet, but Freya didn't mind. She'd think of her friend every time she wore them. Extra thick socks could fill the gap anyway.

Maisie pulled a pair of shoes Freya had admired in a shop window from her bag and slid them onto her feet. She went back to tapping out another routine. On Maisie's other side, Quinn was watching her, apparently keeping time as his feet seemed to move to the same rhythm, although Freya couldn't be positive as she had no musical sense.

Tadgh was back to staring out the window, while Ravi was

once more drawing, this time sketching some of the animals from the wormhole.

"You've nailed it," Freya said.

"Thanks," he mumbled, not looking up.

Freya sighed. She'd nothing to do but stare out the window. A nasty rain had swept up out of nowhere and was now lashing the panes. The temperature on the bus dropped. She longed for a jumper, but her spare one was still damp from the trip to the wormhole.

"You all right?"

Ravi looked concerned.

"Yeah, fine."

"Take this." Ravi slipped out of his jacket and handed it to Freya.

"I can't."

"I don't want it, I'm warm. You can give it back to me when we get to Dublin."

"Thanks."

Freya snuggled into the jacket and watched Ravi sketch.

"You think I've got the bears right?"

"Maybe a little longer on the front paws."

He erased the front paws and drew them a bit longer and rounder.

"Perfect."

"It really happened."

"Yes."

Seamus picked up his megaphone. "Attention, attention, we've only half an hour to Dublin. Time to get your mobiles back. Remember to text your parents, we're due at the bus depot at half four."

Brie was coming down the aisle with her sack, fishing mobile phones and hand held games from the interior as if she was Father Christmas. When she finally arrived at the back row, she smiled at Quinn.

"I think you'll see I've taken very good care of your device."

He smiled. "Knew you would."

Freya raised her eyebrows. How things had changed.

Brie handed Quinn his mobile, which had been wrapped in bubble paper.

"Better than before," he declared.

Everyone but Freya had the latest mobile, although no one else seemed to notice. Until Quinn put out his hands.

"Your mobiles."

They handed them over.

"Going to put myself in your contacts lists."

He punched his number into all their phones. "Here Tadgh, put yours in next."

By the time they slid into the bus depot they had each other's contact info. Maisie had sent a group text with a green heart to ensure they'd started a chat.

The coach screeched to a halt, although not before Freya had caught a glimpse of Quinn's posh car standing out front of the arrivals hall and the crowd that was gathered inside. Freya slipped out of Ravi's jacket and handed it to him.

"Anytime," he said.

The bus driver opened the door as Seamus shouted, "God-speed inmates!"

Everyone tumbled down the aisle, eager to see their families. Freya was in the middle seat, so she had to lead The Misfits off the bus, although she'd have preferred to be the last one off. Every second counted.

Ravi's family was in the hall, his mother holding a large box of Turkish delight, his sister waving. He turned to The Misfits.

"Gonna miss all of you, don't be strangers." He looked at Freya as he said, "You all know where to find The Right Rice."

And with that, he was gone.

"Tadgh!"

The group of twelve rushed to Tadgh, carrying signs that said "welcome back" and "we love you." Tadgh smiled as they surrounded him, burying him with hugs and kisses. He waved at Freya, Maisie and Quinn before the welcoming committee ushered him from the arrivals hall.

Next to go was Quinn. A beautiful woman, looking as if she'd just stepped from the pages of a fashion magazine, smiled with perfect teeth as she strolled toward them. She put her hands on Quinn's shoulders and kissed him, once on each cheek, then smiled at the girls.

"Later," Quinn said.

Freya watched them head toward the posh car. She wondered if the chauffeur would be there again today. She craned her neck. The driver was standing on the pavement in her uniform, arms folded, standing next to the open car door.

"Just…" Maisie began.

The boy Freya had seen Maisie with before had snuck up behind her, putting his hands over her eyes. She laughed.

"Ah Patrick, you missed me."

"Leavin' me alone with Mam and Da? You're not to do that again," Patrick said. He stepped backward.

"Freya, this is my brother Patrick."

"Pleased to meet you." He stuck out his hand. "Come on, Mam'll have my head if we're even five minutes late. She's dyin' to see you."

Maisie gave Freya a quick hug then she and Patrick were on their way.

Freya looked around the arrivals hall. She felt the same

way she had when she was young and it was parents' night to come 'round the school and no one from her family showed.

"Hey there."

Lexie had sidled up next to her. She smiled.

"Let's keep in touch, shall we? I, we've, all been so impressed with you. You've a grand future ahead, Freya. You just need a little help seeing your potential."

Freya rolled her eyes. Now that she'd left St. Dymphna's Holiday Academy, she could see that nothing had changed, would ever change, for her. Lexie's empty words made her feel even more hollow.

"I understand, Freya, I really do. My home life when I went to St. Dymphna's, let's just say no one met me when I got home. You call, text, message, whatever you want. I'll be there. 'kay?" Lexie squeezed her arm. "I'll be in touch. Promise you'll take my calls."

Freya nodded, although she couldn't imagine when or why she'd ever speak to Lexie again. Lexie walked away, joining up with the other green shirts. No doubt they were headed to the nearest pub. Freya headed for the street, dragging her bag. She had to wait a long time for the bus home. She was damp and cold and cross by the time she arrived at the dingy flat. Nora and Allie were screaming so loudly she could hear them from the street. It took a moment for her worn key to open the lock. The twins were elated when she walked through the door. They wrapped their grubby little hands around her legs and smothered her with hugs. Freya smiled. She hadn't realized how much she'd missed them.

"You're back." Mam stood in the doorway, a cigarette in her left hand.

Freya was angry. Madder than she'd ever been.

"Why did you send me away, when I'm coming back to the same life?"

"You're not coming back to the same life." Mam sat on the corner of the ratty blue sofa. "You've come back a new you. Ready to listen to your teachers. To reach potential."

"Reach potential? In this family? At that school?"

Mam blew a smoke ring. "Freya, 'twas the best I could do. I've no money for posh courses or fancy schools. The only way to help you was to send you to that holiday camp."

"Holiday camp." Freya scoffed. "You make it sound like you sent me somewhere for fun. And we both know it wasn't your idea, anyway, it was the nuns."

Mam didn't reply.

"As I thought."

Freya stormed off to her bedroom. She tossed her bag on the floor and sunk down on the mattress. A moment later the twins came running. She played with them for a few minutes, then headed to the kitchen.

"What's for dinner?"

Mam looked up at her with glassy eyes. "Up to you, isn't it?"

SEVENTEEN

Quinn was pleasantly shocked Glynnis had come to fetch him at the bus depot. He was also rather surprised at her effervescent French greeting. Double kisses were hardly a routine part of McMalley family life. Clearly his mother had missed him, though, which filled Quinn with joy. Until they reached the car. At least Glynnis had brought Agnes, his favorite driver, who gave him the sympathetic look she always reserved for Quinn and his siblings when their parents were difficult. She held the door wide and touched his arm while he climbed into the vehicle. Three people he didn't recognize were sitting in the back row, glasses of champagne in their hands.

Glynnis followed Quinn into the middle row and smiled at the others.

"Mon fils, le plus petit. Il s'appelle Quinn," she said in her overly exaggerated French accent.

Quinn sighed. So he was to be his mother's toy this week, the accessory meant to make her look like Super Mam to the French antique dealers who'd come to experience an authentic slice of Ireland. His brothers and sisters had been dragged into this duty before, but Quinn had always been spared the obligation. He wondered what they'd say if they knew he'd just returned from a two-month stint at an academy for at-risk youth. Quinn's French was good enough that he realized his mother was telling them he'd been on the Aran Islands. She made it sound like a fancy holiday. Unfortunately, his French was too poor to correct her assertion. But he was not without resources. For the remainder of the journey to the estate and the duration of their visit, Quinn would ignore them, speaking only in the halting, fractured French he knew Glynnis hated.

When they arrived at their palatial home, Quinn took off for his hives. He'd been so worried the bees would have come to some harm while he was away. Not only were they all fine, they seemed to be thriving. Rodman had pulled through. Quinn breathed a sigh of relief. He'd look into building a new spot for the hive his grandfather would give him on his birthday, based on the space he'd seen at Aine's. Thinking of Aine made him miss Freya, Ravi, Tadgh and most of all Maisie. He'd text her tomorrow to ask how it was being back in the dance studio. Maybe even send her a picture of his hives.

At that very moment, Maisie was thinking of Quinn. She was curious how he was going to manage to get back into training for football after two months away. Her muscle memory had gone soft and her feet were out of practice. Freya's cheap trainers had not had any kind of arch support, and she was afraid she'd have ankle trouble as a result. The past two months had been the most time she'd spent away from a dance studio since she was three. She couldn't wait to feel the floor vibrate and to smell the pomade she used to keep her curls in place.

The instant Maisie and Patrick arrived at the large, semi-d they shared with their parents, she raced to the closet that held her dance shoes. Her fingers shook as she pulled out her favorite pair and slipped them over her feet. Patrick had built her a practice space off the conservatory several years ago, covering the unused potting area with floor boards like the ones in the dance studio. He'd even outfitted the place with a crack sound system, although that was partly so his band could practice there on weekends. Maisie slid one of the DVDs she loved to dance to, crossed her fingers for luck and brushed her feet against the floor. The minute she started to dance, her worries fell away. After half an hour of dancing, she realized it had been an excellent summer. Maisie had discovered she was smarter than she thought and, most important of all, that she was capable in maths. She'd open her dance studio someday, after her years on The Gaiety stage, and no one would ever be able to cheat her out of her earnings.

Ravi also relished returning home. He smiled at the giant box of Turkish delight now sitting on the little table next to his bed. It was the box his mother had presented to him at the bus depot, the one specifically chosen by his father as it was one of the few selections that didn't contain pistachio, which Ravi loathed. Every day he stared at the box, replaying the scene at the station.

His family had been waiting for him in the arrivals hall. No doubt they'd been at least an hour early. Both his parents had a fear that being even a moment late meant losing a potential opportunity. Ravi was pretty certain his mother had wanted to there to greet him to ensure there were no hard feelings about sending him to the holiday academy. She was a firm believer that food, especially treats, were the easiest way to say "I love you." She'd clutched the box of Turkish delight at eye level, no doubt so Ravi would see it straight away as he exited the bus. To her relief, Ravi's face lit up when he saw the sweets.

"Thanks, Mam."

"Not from me. A gift from your father."

Ravi's father smiled. "You have earned it. You took on the challenge of the two months away, and here you are."

"We missed you."

"I missed you, too."

Ravi opened the box. It was full of his favorite flavors, rose and orange. He popped two pieces into his mouth. He'd missed his sweets but the box was big enough to make up for the two- month hiatus.

"Give me your bag."

Ravi's father slung his bag over his shoulder and they walked to the car park.

"Did you get any drawing done?" His mother asked as they drove through the streets of Dublin.

Ravi passed her the tiny notebook he'd carried in his back pocket.

"You have such imagination."

They came to a stoplight. Ravi's mother held up the sketch of the dancing bears so his father could see the drawing.

Ravi's father glanced over at the drawings. He leaned forward, shocked.

"You draw like this?"

"What have I been telling you? Your son is a natural artist."

The light turned green. As Ravi's father pulled into the traffic he said, "You know Ravi, we could use decorations on the walls of the restaurant. Something for people to look at while they wait on their carry-outs."

Ravi's mother smiled at him in the rear-view mirror.

It was four days later, and so many customers at The Right Rice had asked about Ravi's drawings that his father had suggested maybe Ravi could have a hand at drawing a new logo for the carry-out menu. Ravi hoped Freya would come by the shop so she could see them, but so far she'd been a no-show. He was afraid to invite her, since it might have seemed a bit much, so he just settled for liking the two posts she'd put up on her socials.

The socials. What a nightmare. When Freya finally had the chance to wrestle the twins into a nap she decided to look her new friends up online. Quinn, as she suspected, was from one of Dublin's poshest families, with ties to France, Italy and Switzerland. His eldest sister was some sort of fashion muse, which wasn't a surprise, given what she'd seen of his elegant mother. He went to one of the elite feeder schools that sent its graduates off to the most reputable unis in Europe and the States. His pages were full of himself attending all kinds of sport events, in private boxes, posing with some of the world's top athletes.

Tadgh, to her surprise, was in the same league. Although he didn't have his own accounts, except for one with twelve followers, he appeared fairly frequently on the pages of his siblings. The photos showed him in one of the gorgeous, castle like houses south of Dublin, overlooking the sea. He was riding horses, walking big dogs, on vacation on a yacht. Freya had been wrong to worry about Tadgh. He would do just fine.

Freya bit her lip. She had always prided herself on not being the jealous type. Now she realized she'd never before encountered people who had so many of the things she coveted. Every one of her St. Dymphna's Holiday Academy friends was more of a winner than she would ever be. They had friends and families who loved them. They belonged.

She sent out a text to the group, reminding them of their last dive. Tadgh and Ravi liked her message, but didn't offer any additional words. Maisie and Quinn didn't even reply.

Maisie was the one who most surprised Freya. She'd acted as though they were similar, when the reality was Maisie was far more like the clique who'd been in Freya's cabin. No wonder, Freya thought bitterly, none of the girls had disliked Maisie. Almost all of the photos on Maisie's socials showed her surrounded by a group of girls, some of them fellow step dancers, others just clearly her friends. She was a champion step dancer and clearly her family was loaded. No wonder she thought she'd own a dance studio one day.

Ravi was of course most like her, but even he had his surprises. One day Freya walked past The Right Rice. She saw Ravi inside, laughing, as he packed up a carry-out bag. His drawing of the bears in the wormhole hung in a frame on the wall behind him. The boys and girl getting their food seemed familiar. After they paid, the guy with the dirty blonde hair high-fived Ravi. As they turned to leave the shop, Freya realized it was Maisie, Quinn and Tadgh.

EIGHTEEN

Freya cried herself to sleep. The new term started in a week and she'd nothing to look forward to. Maisie, Quinn, Ravi and Tadgh sent occasional group texts, which she always liked, but no one offered to get together. Freya never suggested meeting up since it was clear she was a one-euro sliced roll girl, while they were all able to afford restaurant carry-out. She was certain they were meeting up behind her back. Several of the photos on Ravi and Maisie's posts seemed to be from the same location. She tortured herself with questions about what she'd done wrong. Why she was always on the outside. Mam was right. No one wanted to be around her. Not even her own father.

The misfits weren't the only ones Freya cyberstalked. She'd gone onto the pages of the mean cabin mates, who, as she had guessed all seemed to know each other. And then there were the St. Dymphna's Holiday Academy counselors. They were also far different in real life than on the Aran Islands. Lexie was a tech worker at Silicon Docks, while Brie worked in a lab at Trinity College and Seamus was a drink and drug rehab counselor. She'd had a laugh at that, imagining him scaring people straight.

The night before the new term started, Freya couldn't contain her anxiety. It was hard to contemplate facing the nuns who'd had her sent to St. Dymphna's against her will. Even though it had been by far the best summer of her life, she still felt betrayed. Why didn't they just ask for her consent? No one ever listened to Freya. She was invisible. It was to be another year of eating lunch alone, hunched over her books, pretending she didn't care.

She paced the floor. Yelled at the twins with such force that they sat quietly on the couch with their toys. Wondered if she'd be better off dropping out of school, though she knew that wasn't really a possibility. She imagined herself living on Inis Mor, having tea with Aine and playing with the bears in the wormhole. She missed Aine terribly. Several times she'd tried to find her, looking up information on Inis Mor and record keepers, but she'd come up empty.

Her phone buzzed.

Lexie.

Freya sighed. She had been dodging Lexie's calls for a while now. When she'd first returned to Dublin, she'd spoken with her a few times. But she always felt so sad afterwards. There was no point. Lexie had tried, but nothing in Freya's world had changed. She stared at her phone. Normally she would never answer. Tonight, with Mam slumped over in the sitting room and the first day of a new school year looming large, Freya was dying to talk to someone over the age of four.

"Hello."

"I've been thinking about you, Freya. Are you set with going back tomorrow? Have everything you need in your supply bag?"

Freya scoffed. She never had the supplies she needed. The

nuns had "care bags" for the girls whose families couldn't afford pens, protractors, notebooks and uniforms. The care bags were kept in a locked cupboard. It was humiliating to have to ask for the key every time her pencil broke or she ran out of paper, but Freya had no choice.

"You're having one off on me, right?" Freya was disgusted.

"No, of course not. I'm sorry things are not great in your world." Lexie took a deep breath, "We failed you. Let me make things right."

"Failed me?"

"Yep, we blew it. You're more despondent than when you came to us. That's not our mission."

"I don't know what you're talking about." Freya's back tightened.

"You have a lot of potential. But it's being wasted."

"Tell me something I don't already know."

"How would you like to go to another school?"

"We don't have money for fees."

"I know. I'm aware of your situation. My mother's on the board of trustees of one of the top girls' schools here in Dublin."

Freya rolled her eyes. Was Lexie trying to impress her?

"Good for you, I guess," Freya said cautiously.

"My mother endowed a scholarship fund for promising girls in STEM. You know, science, tech, engineering and maths. The girl who has the scholarship this year is leaving in the middle of the year, at the end of term. The scholarship will be available then. It's for use at the prep school of your choice, although I recommend my alma mater."

"I don't understand what you're saying."

"I've a scholarship you can use to attend the school of your choice, after the Christmas holidays."

"That's nice, but I can't afford a trip on the LUAS. No way I could ever travel to any school beyond walking distance."

"The scholarship covers tuition, meals, uniforms, supplies and all travel expenses. Transport to and from school as well as all school holiday travel."

"People travel on school holidays?"

"Yes, to some very cool places. Last year one of the schools from here in Dublin went on a dig of Roman ruins in the south of France. You'd need a passport, of course, but even that's not a problem, because scholarship funds cover everything. Let me put your name up for consideration. Come on, Freya, what do you have to lose?"

"When can I start?" Freya's heart felt like it was beating on the other side of her skin.

"We'll get you your reading list in mid-autumn. The first day of classes will be in January, after the Christmas holidays. There's only one catch."

Freya collapsed onto the frayed armchair. She should have known not to let her hopes rise.

"It's a small one, but I need to show you've demonstrated leadership potential. Normally the admissions committee requires that prospective students have a wide range of outside interests and accomplishments."

Freya bit her lip. She'd never had the time for any kind of extracurricular activities. And the schools she attended were not exactly bursting with options.

"That's it then, it's not going to work...."

"Don't worry, I've got you covered. The Misfits Club."

Freya narrowed her eyes. "What about The Misfits Club?"

"I read the ideas proposed for the club. Very fresh and original. I'll help you bring the club to life, establish a bit of credibility. You'll be sure to be awarded the scholarship."

Freya sighed. "The club wasn't just my idea."

"You and I know that, but you're the one who needs the ticket to a better place."

"I don't know."

"Look, everyone else is doing fine. Thriving since they've come back from Inis Mor."

Freya's chest tightened. "You've talked to them?"

"Oh yes, several times. Even Tadgh."

Freya felt like she'd been punched in the stomach. It was an effort to take a deep breath. So they had been ghosting her. Still, if there was one thing Freya prided herself on it was honesty. She'd have to get their okay if she wanted to take the idea of the club public.

"Okay," Freya said slowly, "I just have to be sure it's okay with the others."

"Freya, for once in your life, let yourself and your future matter."

As soon as she got off the phone with Lexie Freya sent a text to the group.

Can I use the idea for The Misfits Club as part of a school application?

Have at it Quinn responded immediately.

Best of luck Ravi wrote.

Tadgh gave the idea a thumbs up.

Maisie didn't respond at all, which Freya found to be no surprise. She'd been watching Maisie's stories, trying to tamp down her jealousy. Maisie was off in dance land, readying herself for a slew of competitions. Freya watched Maisie twirl around stages, some as far away as London, wearing pricey shoes and dresses that must have cost a fortune while Freya was stuck wearing extra thick socks to make the trainers Maisie had stretched fit her narrow feet. Although she missed them all, she was most hurt by Maisie's apathy. She'd been certain she had finally made a close girlfriend. Mam had always told her she couldn't get along with a group of girls. Freya had assumed she could have at least one friend. Maisie proved her wrong.

The new school term was bearable, now that Freya knew she wouldn't be there for long. She forced herself to be polite to the nuns. She couldn't afford for them to call her disagreeable or her scholarship could be in danger.

Lexie was pleased she'd convinced Freya to promote The Misfits Club. She'd been so sad when she realized Freya's time at St. Dymphna had not improved her life. She'd searched for weeks for a way to help Freya. The scholarship opening was perfect.

"How is this going to work?" Freya asked her the next afternoon on the phone.

"I've found some environmental podcasts looking for guests. You'll come on to be interviewed…"

"I can't do that," Freya said.

"Why not?"

"I have to watch my sisters."

"Stick them in front of the telly for twenty minutes and they'll be grand. You're going to do the interviews from home. Easy peasy. I'll help with the set-up. Install the mic. You'll be good to go."

The following Wednesday, Lexie arrived in the late afternoon, armed with everything Freya would need for a podcast. She even brought sweets for the twins to snack on while Freya was on air. Mam was on her best behavior, acting as if her daughter being interviewed was an everyday event.

"Now remember," Lexie instructed, "There's to be no mention of St. Dymphna's."

Freya nodded. She knew the rules.

"Right then, best of luck tomorrow!"

Freya was nervous. The podcast would be live. Everything she said would go out into cyberspace, stored forever somewhere on the internet. It was a lot of pressure.

Lexie had told her to do the podcast from the bathroom. "Acoustics," she'd said, as if Freya had any notion of what that meant.

When the time came for the podcast, Freya crossed her fingers for luck, pumped the twins full of sweets and dragged the mic to the bathroom.

"Three, two, one and we're live!" The interviewer said from across Dublin.

Freya smiled. It was the most exciting moment of her life.

NINETEEN

Tadgh missed his friends. Every day he thought about his time in St. Dymphna's. How he had been accepted for who he was. No one there crossed the street when they saw him coming, or thought it was odd he sometimes talked to himself. Mam and Da and his brothers and sisters did their best, but they always looked like they were holding their breath, waiting for the moment he'd say or do something wrong. Most of the time Tadgh didn't know what he'd done that was so unacceptable. He only knew he made people nervous.

That was one of the reasons he had no socials. He was aware people didn't understand when you were slagging them off online. They got very angry when they thought they'd been slighted.

And now the same thing was happening with his new friends. Freya had sent that text asking if she could use The Misfits Club, which he didn't understand. Use the club for what? He'd been so excited that day on the trip to Inis Mor, when he'd called them The Misfits Club. And then, when they wanted to use the name for the conservation project, he'd felt he'd earned another stamp of approval. But now Freya was taking the club for herself. He wanted to ask Quinn and Ravi what they thought, but he couldn't imagine how to word his text.

It had been so fantastic to see them that day in downtown, when he'd dropped by The Right Rice to pick up a curry on his way home. Quinn and Maisie had been in the take-away line when he arrived. Right away he'd wondered if they'd been together, or just run into each other. Ravi had been so excited to show everyone the drawings hanging on the walls of the restaurant.

No one had mentioned Freya at all, which was odd. Tadgh hadn't thought anything of it at the time, but now, with this news Freya was going to use The Misfits Club for herself, he wondered if they'd decided she was no longer their friend.

Tadgh had tried to interest Ravi and Quinn in getting together, but Ravi had been busy filling up little metal containers with curry and Quinn had been busy staring at Maisie. It was sad, Tadgh thought, the way friends fell like leaves from a tree during a windstorm.

Fully recovered from no studio time for two months?

Maisie smiled when she saw the text from Quinn.

Almost. Yourself?

Maybe.

Maisie and Quinn discovered they had a few common friends. Several of the girls from her dance studio traveled up from Quinn's neighborhood, and Patrick had played a few gigs for some friends of Quinn's sisters. Quinn's football team had a number of practices near her dance studio. They ran into each other on the street several times, then began to make a habit of getting together. Both attended high pressure schools and parents who expected a lot.

"You get me," Quinn said one day as they were crossing St. Stephen's Green.

"Same," Maisie replied. She took a deep breath. "I've a big feis coming up. If I place, I may end up on the best competitive team."

"I'll be there," Quinn said. "Cheer you on."

"Really?"

"Sure."

Maisie smiled.

She'd wanted to invite all the misfits to come, but she was afraid it would be awkward. After they'd returned to Dublin, Freya had been very distant. She didn't even watch all of Maisie's stories. Maisie was sad, since she really liked Freya. She was on her phone, about to message Freya to ask if she wanted to meet up, when Patrick grabbed it from her hand.

"Feis time." He held it over her head. "You'll get it back after the competition."

Maisie nodded. She couldn't afford the distraction. Her computer already had built in blocks to keep her off the socials. It was rough but it would be worth it when she took first place. And, now that Quinn had all the details about the feis, there was no one she'd need to speak with anyway.

"What does it mean to be a misfit?" The interviewer demanded.

"That you don't have a place. You're on the other side of the glass, waving, hoping someone will notice you, but they can't see you because the pane is frosted."

"That's brilliant. Who hasn't felt like that?"

Freya rolled her eyes. From her vantage point, she suspected most of the people she knew had never felt that way. Or if they had, they'd commiserated about it with their friends, which of course meant they weren't really outsiders at all.

"Now this club. Where did you get the idea for it?"

Freya took a deep breath. She felt guilty not mentioning Maisie, Quinn, Ravi or Tadgh, but she knew there was no way to name them unless she talked about St. Dymnphna's, which was forbidden.

"I was thinking about endangered animals. How they're misfits, the way they don't fit in with their environments. Like people who don't belong."

The minute the words left her mouth, Freya realized she was parroting Tadgh. Was it plagiarism if you spoke someone else's words? She felt terribly guilty.

"So the club is to help animals reconnect with their environments."

"We make it possible to reconnect, by cleaning the beaches and parks and woods so animals can be in their habitats."

Of course this was all a theory. But the interviewer didn't need to know it. Lexie was confident that once Freya put the idea out there for The Misfits Club, people would take it upon themselves to form their own groups.

"Now that is smart. Tell me, are there any rules for the club?"

"Yes. No leaders, no slagging off other members and no grown-ups."

"Now that is a club I'd love to have belonged to," the interviewer said. "You heard it here first, my lovelies. Go forth and create your own Misfits Clubs."

Freya was sweating by the time the interview ended. The minute she was off the air, Lexie rang.

"Brilliant! You were incredible!"

"Thanks."

"Tell me, do you have all your socials updated?"

"My socials?" Freya was horrified.

It was embarrassing, to have so few followers.

"Found you here, well done Freya! Very few friends and followers. Clearly you're very selective."

"I ... sure."

"We may want to see you go on a few more platforms."

"Why?"

"Trust me. I think you're about to create a movement."

Freya was sure Lexie was wrong, but she didn't want to disappoint her, and she'd agreed to do everything requested. So she created accounts on all the major social platforms. Lexie was her only friend and follower half an hour later, when she'd turned off her phone and headed to the kitchen with the twins.

When she woke up the next morning, The Misfits Club was trending.

TWENTY

Freya never wanted to be famous. She'd never understood why so many people her age wanted to be influencers. Not when there were maths problems to solve and scientific theories to contemplate and books to read. She had zero tolerance for people who spent hours on their phones, rearranged themselves for the perfect shot to post, and hung on to every like. None of it mattered at all. Until the day she blew up.

It was the podcast, along with being tagged in a photo of a dirty beach with dead animals that was posted by one of Lexie's connected tech friends. By the time Freya finished her morning tea, her accounts held thousands of followers. Every time she refreshed, there were more names on the list. Suddenly people cared about her, and what she thought. Her DMs were overflowing with requests to appear on podcasts.

The Misfits have gone viral!!!

Freya sent the text to Maisie, Quinn, Ravi and Tadgh, along with a screen shot of her new social media followers tally, shortly before noon. By half-three, she was beginning to wonder if her mobile service had cut out, although her social numbers were still climbing. She sent the text again. Finally, Ravi responded.

No more followers for me. Same old same old.

Same.

Ditto.

She clicked the feeds of Ravi, Quinn and Maisie. Sure enough, they had the same low number of followers as before. Tadgh, as predicted, had only a small account that was private.

Tadgh sent a text that read **Don't understand.**

Neither did Maisie, Quinn or Ravi. Until Patrick, who was a keen follower of all things trending, found the interview Freya had done the day before. He forwarded it to Maisie, who posted it to the others.

Betrayed.

Tadgh's one-word text said it all. Freya had sold them out.

"I had no idea," Maisie practically wept the next day. "I thought we were friends."

They had agreed to meet at The Right Rice after school. They sat at a table in the far corner, beneath Ravi's drawing of the auks.

Ravi squeezed her arm. "Maybe it's a big misunderstanding."

"We can only hope so," Maisie replied.

Quinn didn't say anything. He was disgusted but not surprised. He'd seen his parents undercut their competitors far too many times to count. He'd also, if he was honest, made a few questionable football moves over the years.

"Let's give her a chance," Ravi said.

Tadgh nodded. He had clearly been fighting hard not to cry. Quinn and Ravi exchanged looks. They'd need to make more of an effort with Tadgh.

Across Dublin, Freya was almost doubled over with guilt. She had taken all the credit for an idea that wasn't even hers.

There was only one way to make things right. She'd have to out the others as co-creators of The Misfits Club.

She turned on her phone. Her feed was flooded with photos of kids cleaning beaches, parks and woodlands. On five continents. Her phone pinged. Make that six continents. Hashtags referencing The Misfits Club appeared on all their pictures. The Misfits Club was officially a global phenomenon.

Fantastic news. Lexie texted.

I can't keep claiming this club is mine.

Freya's phone rang.

"It's me, Lexie. Listen, it would be grand if you could do a few more podcasts. Really cement your spot, so you're not just flavor of the day. Plus, it would benefit the animals."

"I'll text everyone…"

"That's not what I am asking."

Freya frowned. The Misfits Club belonged equally to all five of The Misfits.

"It's just not right, what I'm doing."

"Look Freya, I know how these things work. There can only be one spokesperson. And you're it!"

"I don't know, maybe the others would like to be interviewed. We could split any appearances."

"Didn't you hear me, Freya? Every group has one major spokesperson."

Freya looked over at the twins, who were slathering bits of buttered macaroni into each other's hair. She sighed. It was going to take forever to clean them and their clothes and the floor.

"There is only room for one boss."

"Not true! My sisters are twins. Mam says they're a package deal."

"Answer me honestly, you know there is one who is the boss."

Nora was pointing at the bowl of mac and cheese. Allie picked up a spoon and awkwardly tried to feed her sister. It had always been that way, Nora making the orders, Allie doing the work.

"You're right. One boss."

"Don't worry. Your friends will be pleased. You've achieved your common goal of bringing awareness to the danger to the animals. And you've shown that kids, without any grownups, make a difference. You're letting the other misfits know they matter."

"I still think the others might want to be on the podcasts."

"Listen to me, Freya. You can't have Tadgh do a live interview. What would happen if he froze up? He'd be traumatized. I don't think you'd feel right, putting him in the spotlight. Too much stress. It wouldn't be right to have all the others but one. No, it makes more sense to have just you as the face of the club."

Freya sighed. She didn't like Lexie slagging Tadgh, but it was true. There was no way he'd want to be in front of a lot of people. And Maisie and Ravi and Quinn would all be sorry to be pulled away from the dance studio, the notepad and the beehives. At least that's what Freya told herself. By the time she logged on to do the next set of interviews Lexie had lined up, Freya had herself completely convinced she was doing the group a favor. Taking care of things on behalf of everyone so they could spend their precious hours after school and on weekends as they wished. In fact, they should be thanking her. She was doing all the heavy lifting while they were off enjoying their free time.

Freya was convinced that Lexie knew everything there was to know about interviews and social media. If she said The Misfits Club would be best represented by one person, she must be right. She practiced annunciating as she fed and bathed the twins.

She was still annoyed not to have heard from The Misfits. She sent a new text, with a link to the interviews Lexie had scheduled.

Maisie, Ravi and Tadgh were livid. Quinn was so angry he picked up the phone.

"You what?" Quinn practically shouted.

He called almost exactly a minute after the podcast aired. The taping had been a bit of a blur. Freya had been very nervous. All her life Mam had been telling her to pipe down, that no one was interested in hearing what she thought. Yet here she was, people eager to hear her opinion on loads of subjects. She'd even been asked her views on the latest trio of buskers on Grafton Street. It was quite addictive. She had been thrilled when Quinn called. Finally, someone who would want to celebrate the podcast with her.

Freya was shocked at his rage, sure Quinn sounded angrier over the phone than he would have been in person. Even when she'd seen him angry at some of the other St. Dymphna's campers for mocking Tadgh, he hadn't used the tone he took with Freya.

"I thought …."

"No, you didn't think. Or maybe more to the point, all you thought about was Freya. I can't believe you didn't mention any of us. 'The Misfits Club,' you couldn't even give Tadgh credit for creating the name. The animals, the clean-ups, the no grown-ups allowed. It was the Freya show."

Freya bit her lip. Clearly it was not the time to tell Quinn Lexie had suggested she start her own group, called "Freya's Friends." She sighed at the irony. Thanks to the podcast, she had no friends.

TWENTY-ONE

Maisie, Quinn, Ravi and Tadgh met up for lunch on St. Stephen's Green one sunny autumn afternoon. Maisie came straight from the studio, her dance shoes slung across her shoulders. She had been dancing better than ever since coming back from Inis Mor, which was rather strange. Despite taking the longest break she'd had since she was four, Maisie was stronger than if she'd been practicing ten hours a day. Even better, she was now middle of the class in maths. All of her worries had smoothed over, except her concern about Freya.

"Do you think we didn't really know her?" Maisie plopped down on the grass next to Quinn.

Ravi, who was normally so laid back, erupted. "I can't believe she'd do this, take over everything."

Maisie picked up a blade of grass. She was thinking about how Freya had never gotten the chance to take dance lessons or pursue anything she wanted. Instead, she was like a miniature mother. Of twins. Maisie had once done a babysitting gig, for her uncle's next door neighbor, and it was awful. She'd lasted three hours before she'd called Mam, crying, begging to be rescued. And that had been with only one little girl in her charge.

"Maybe she just needed to be seen. We all had problems, obviously. But she was the saddest person at St. Dymphna's."

Quinn shook his head. "You're too nice."

Maisie blushed.

"Seriously what Freya did is wrong. Ever done a group project at school and when it's time to turn it in the person who did the least signs their name first?"

"I don't think she did the least amount of work," Ravi said.

"I'm not saying she did, but she didn't do anything that made her spokesperson. The Misfits Club is for all the misfits. There is no star. That's the whole point of the group."

Tadgh frowned. "It's not right we're here without her, we didn't give her a chance. She could explain."

"You mean she didn't give us a chance." Ravi tried to put on a brave front, but the others heard the hurt in his voice. "Just up and left us."

"Has anyone talked to her lately?"

"I invited her to the feis. I never got a response."

"Not cool," Quinn said. "Especially since we'll all be there."

Ravi sighed. He'd longed to text Freya, but she'd been so different with that last text. So full of herself. Pleased about going viral. Clearly he'd been mistaken when he thought she didn't care about likes.

"Maybe she's just one of those holiday people. The ones who were very different when they're away. When my parents take us back to India, even when my grandparents or aunts and uncles came to stay in Dublin, we don't recognize our mother or our father. They act like completely different people."

"Well then who is the real Freya? The girl we thought we knew in Inis Mor or the popularity obsessed podcaster in Dublin?"

No one answered Quinn's question.

Ravi was pretty certain the Inis Mor version was the real Freya, but he didn't want to make a fool of himself, so he decided to continue liking all her posts while waiting for the day she'd slide into his DMs. Lately it seemed like it was going to be a long wait.

"You know she's going to be on RTE."

"I heard she'd doing The Late Show."

Ravi sighed. He knew they'd all enjoy being part of those programs. It was wrong of Freya to hog all of the opportunities.

"I thought she liked us." Tadgh was solemn. "All she talks about is the club."

"Like it's her club." Maisie couldn't explain it, but hearing the others lit a fire in her. She was much more irritated by Freya the longer they talked. "She sold us out."

"I don't know…."

"Face it, Ravi, it's clear. Want a scone?"

Ravi wasn't so sure. Until the following week, when news broke of Freya's latest triumph. She'd appeared, in person, on a late night chat show. The host asked if there were any others she wanted to credit for The Misfits Club. She'd hesitated a moment. He'd held his breath. Leaned forward, waiting for her to mention them. But she'd sat in silence. It was the last straw. Ravi's finger hovered over her photo for a moment before he clicked the delete button.

Freya had a feeling they were meeting up without her. It was the story of her life. She'd get in with a group of people and somehow she'd do something wrong and all of a sudden she was on the outs. At least she had the blogs and the guest appearances.

It would be such an honor to be on RTE. She was only sorry she would be there alone. She busied herself in the hour before the interview, looking through her phone. There had been so many messages. She'd scrolled right past them, often distracted by Nora and Allie and now trying to fit in the reading list for her new school. It was official as of last week. The thick envelope had been stuck in the mail slot when she arrived home. A full scholarship, to a school where others cared about maths and physics and all things scientific. She was overjoyed. Until she realized there was no one to share her good news.

Lexie had given her a congratulatory card, which she'd taped to the cracked mirror in her bedroom. Mam had said that now Freya was admitted, she'd better be sure to stay on her toes so the twins could one day attend as well. It wasn't exactly the well done message she'd hoped for, but it was better than nothing.

Right before she went on air, Freya saw it.

Miss you terribly. Please come to my feis.

She didn't know how she hadn't seen the message before, although she suspected it was because she'd been so busy reading all the admiring DMs.

"On in three, two, one..."

Freya threw back her shoulders. There was something she needed to do. Should she wait to be asked, or bring it up herself? She shuffled her feet across the floor, doing the dance step Maisie had showed her in Inis Mor. She was ready.

"My guest today needs no introduction. She single-handedly started an environmental movement that's gone global. All around the world, teams of kids calling themselves The Misfits are cleaning and clearing beaches, parks, woodlands, gardens, parking lots. You name it and one of the misfits has claimed it, made it more habitable for our animal friends and maybe, just maybe, crossed an entry or two off the endangered species list. Please help me welcome our friend Freya!"

"Thanks, Charlie. And thank you to all the misfits around the world. I have to correct you, though."

"Oh?"

"Yes. You said I single-handedly started an environmental movement. That's not true. The Misfits Club was started by four friends and myself. We all love animals and were gutted to see so many species in danger of disappearing. You look around … lots of the birds flying over Ireland may be making their final journeys. We came up with the idea for the club to show people our age can make a difference. All the grown-ups, well let's just say there's a lot of talk and very little action."

The host laughed. "Here, here. And don't get me started about some of our betters lecturing us about climate changes from the tarmac, aboard their private jets."

"I don't know anything about that, and it doesn't matter. The Misfits Club is a place for everyone to belong. Maisie, Quinn, Ravi, Tadgh and myself. We all formed the group."

"Well done all of you. We need to pause for a commercial break."

Freya rubbed her palms together. She was afraid Lexie was going to call, tell her what a mistake she'd made, maybe even rescind the scholarship. But it didn't matter. The stone of guilt that had been sitting atop her heart was gone.

"Welcome back! Freya give us your best suggestions for

making our homes and our country more hospitable for our animal companions...."

Freya recited her usual list. When the interview was over, she was asked if there was anyone she wanted to acknowledge. She took a deep breath.

"Hi to Mam and Nora and Allie and Da. And most of all, Maisie, Quinn, Ravi and Tadgh."

There was the usual mountain of fan mail on the front hall floor when she got home from her big interview. Letters from all over the world had been making their way to her, by way of Lexie, who had offered her own address up for Freya's safety.

She reached for the new envelopes. Some of them bore stamps she'd never seen. Most of them just said "Freya" on the front, or "The Misfits Club." She slid her finger across the top of one from The Philippines and pulled out the letter.

Dear Freya, Thank you for giving me hope. I'm the only girl in my village interested in maths and science and animals. I always thought I was a freak but you've made me realize I'm just different. And smart. Just like you. I'm starting a Misfits Club with my brother and my best friend. We're going to clean up the beach this weekend and leave water out for all the animals.

Your friend, Jasmine

"Another admirer?" Freya's mother stood in the door, a carrier bag swinging from her left arm. The two whiskey bottles inside the sack clinked together.

Freya frowned. "Mam, you have to stop. With me gone at school across town, who will watch the girls?"

"So now you're calling me a deadbeat mother, are you? Very cheeky my girl. By the way, I heard you. On RTE. Not bad."

Freya brightened. "Really?"

"Sure, you know what you're doing all right."

This was high praise. Freya smiled.

"Still, 'tis not your place to police me. I'll have you know these bottles are for the party I'm throwing tomorrow night."

"Really?" Freya was thrilled. Her mother never had guests. She was certain Mam would be a lot less mean if only she had a few friends.

"You started a club, why shouldn't I?"

Freya bit her lip. So her mother was hosting a drinking group. Still it was better than nothing.

"It's a book group. We've read a novel about an environmentalist who goes on safari and finds herself."

"That's great."

Freya's mother backed up until she was sitting on the crooked steps that led to their upstairs neighbor's flat. "It's thanks to you. I know I don't say it much, but I'm proud of you, Freya. You're livin' up to your potential. I'm proud of us both, if I hadn't the wherewithal to send you to St. Dymphna's none of this would have happened."

It was hard for Freya not to roll her eyes. Her mother always took credit for everything, like the sun rising in the morning or the Liffey filling after a rainstorm. It was so annoying when no one else got any credit. Like mother like daughter, she realized with a start.

"Thanks, Mam."

"Don't forget Freya, you'll be needed to mind the girls when I've my party."

Freya rushed to her room and grabbed her phone. She

found a link to the interview and pasted it in, along with the text she sent to The Misfits.

Chat in one hour. Please.

After she pressed the send button, Freya held her breath. She'd done the best she could. The rest was up to the others.

TWENTY-TWO

Quinn ignored his buzzing phone. He was much more interested in the buzzing of his hives. After he returned from St. Dymphna's his grandfather had been so impressed with Quinn's newfound sense of responsibility that he gave him two hives of endangered bees. Quinn took his stewardship duties seriously.

"Darling, I'm afraid you're spending all your time with the hives. Why don't you ever get together with your friends anymore?"

Quinn rolled his eyes before turning to face his mother.

"Seriously? You don't like anything I do. Nothing. I'd have thought that after St. Dymphna's you'd have missed me."

Glynnis's big blue eyes were overcome with tears. "Oh Quinn, it's quite the opposite. You're my baby. Don't tell the others but you've always been my favorite."

Quinn cocked his head. He was pretty sure that if there was a mothering handbook, this would be against the rules.

Glynnis nodded. "Do you know how hard it's been, watching you fail to show up for yourself? You've more potential than the rest of them combined. But you've always been your own man. I've tried to help you harness yourself, but I've failed. I don't know how to deal with someone who makes the rules instead of following them. I'm very proud of you."

"You have an odd way of showing it. Hassling me about my hives. And my friends."

"I just don't want you to be alone. I've watched you retreat into yourself...."

Quinn laughed.

"What's so funny?"

"You! I am lost in my life. Doing what I want."

Glynnis wiped her eyes.

"Don't worry about me. I promise. But if you'll excuse me, my friends are texting."

Glynnis blew Quinn a kiss.

He removed the protective glove he wore around the hives and pulled the phone from his pocket. Freya. A group chat would be a chance to talk with Maisie. He hadn't seen her in two weeks.

Down to talk.

On the other side of the Liffey, Ravi was stacking boxes in the storeroom so he could draw the odd angles they made when leaned against the crooked wall beneath the stairs. He was surprised to get the message from Freya and kind of disappointed she wanted a group chat. He'd been so sure she liked him the way he liked her, until the night she'd been interviewed on telly and she'd forgotten to mention him and the others. But at least she wanted to communicate. Ravi put a thumbs up on the message and got back to his drawing.

While Ravi was sketching and Quinn beekeeping, Maisie was also knee deep in her passion. Literally. She was lying on the wooden floor of the dance studio, her knees pointing to the sky, her ankles askew. She'd just fallen after one of her easiest jumps. She was already shocked that she'd taken a tumble. It had been a long while since she'd struggled with sticking a landing. Her phone buzzed. Gingerly Maisie sat up, rubbing her ankle as she reached for it.

"Let me get that for you." Arabella handed Maisie her bag.

Maisie looked at the text, followed the link and wept. She couldn't remember the last time she'd cried so hard.

"Just a swollen foot, girl, you'll be right as rain before you know it."

Maisie wiped her eyes. "'tis is a happy cry."

"The best kind."

Patrick was already on the pavement outside the dance studio. "Did you see it? The interview?"

Maisie nodded.

He set out his arm and helped her toward the car. Halfway down the pavement, Maisie yelled, "Wait!"

She put a heart around the video and the invitation to chat.

In. I am all in.

When they got home, Patrick led Maisie to the back garden. He lugged out his laptop and they watched the interview again. Maisie couldn't stop her happy cry.

"Like I've been saying, you need your maths. Dancing may not be a permanent career."

She looked at her phone. Thirty-eight minutes until the chat. She had just enough time for a cuppa and a bite of the Turkish delight Ravi had given her when they'd last met up. She knew he was going to be ecstatic. He'd never stopped believing in Freya.

A new message appeared on her phone screen.

Can't believe I missed the feis. Thanks a mil for the invite. Hope you placed.

Freya hadn't ditched her after all.

Thirty kilometers south, on a sunny terrace overlooking the sea, Tadgh counted down the minutes until the chat. He'd missed his friends terribly. It was almost cruel to discover what he'd been lacking all these years. Every day he checked his messages, eager for another group chat. But the others had gone on with their lives. Maisie was quite good about texting him almost every week, but their conversations were short, and it wasn't the same thing as hanging out in person. Finally, another group get together. He'd have preferred to have it in person, but clearly the others had real life friends, so cyber buddies they would have to be. He topped off his lemonade and wondered what he should say when they asked what he'd been doing. Perhaps they'd like to hear about his life in Bray, the record he'd set on the arcade machine or the funny day trippers from Dublin. He grabbed the pen and paper sitting on the table next to him and jotted down a few ideas so he'd be ready if he got the chance.

Freya was shocked they'd all agreed to the chat. She'd been half afraid they'd ghost her. Not Tadgh, since he was loyal to a fault. But Quinn and Maisie, well she wasn't so sure. And Ravi. It still hurt, how much she missed him. Several times she'd walked past The Right Rice, hoping to catch sight of him through the window. Once he'd been handing over a carry-out meal to a woman in a bright pink sari. She'd watched from behind a tree across the street, aching to go inside the shop, knowing she couldn't. At least today she'd hear what he'd been up to since they'd left St. Dymphna's.

Her phone alarm pinged. Freya smiled to herself, then logged on. To her horror, she was the only one on the chat.

"Mam! Help! Help me!"

Tadgh's mother rushed onto the veranda. He was sitting in one of the wide wicker chairs facing the sea, holding his phone. She let out a breath of relief when she found he wasn't hurt.

"What is it, love?"

He held up his phone. "I can't get a signal. Group chat. Now."

Tadgh's mother realized the importance of the moment. She dashed out of the room, to the study at the far end of the hall. Quickly she rooted through the massive antique desk, quite the irony she'd purchased it from that boy Quinn's mother, until she found the small black box. Tadgh was wailing as she returned to the veranda. She plugged the device into the wall, once again thankful the builder had insisted they spring for an electrical outlet on the terrace.

"Try your mobile now."

Tadgh toggled the device. "It works!"

"Mobile hot spot, good for several hours. Enjoy your chat." She kissed the top of his head then retreated to the other side of the house.

Tadgh!

He smiled seeing his name.

Hey Freya.

A moment later they were joined by Maisie, Quinn and Ravi. Freya was so happy she almost wept.

My friends can you ever know how sorry I am.

We know. Maisie responded. Although she wasn't certain the boys would agree, she didn't think they would argue.

Glam star.

Freya put up a laughing emoji in response to Quinn's message. Clearly he wasn't mad anymore.

You're always my friend.

She put a heart over Tadgh's message, then stared at the screen. Ravi had still not responded, but he was on the chat. If there was one thing Freya had learned in life, it was to ask for what you wanted. The worst that could happen was someone could say no. She'd once heard an old man say it wasn't the failures in life that haunted a person, it was the chances one was too afraid to take.

Made any new drawings Ravi?

Still no reply.

Freya sighed.

Many sketches.

Freya smiled. **Post them. Please.**

Ravi put up two drawings of the stock room of The Right Rice.

Cool.

Freya was annoyed Maisie beat her to the chance to praise the drawings. Until she remembered how lucky she was her friends were speaking to her at all.

Miss you all. Feel terrible.

In the past Quinn responded.

I miss St. Dymphna's.

Of course Tadgh would miss the holiday academy. He thrived on routine. And he was used to being bullying. Freya chided herself – these were not very kind things to think about a kind person like Tadgh.

We should go back.

Freya rolled her eyes. Now Tadgh had gone too far. But to her surprise, the others put hearts around the text.

A fortnight 'til midterm holidays. Tadgh texted.

Give me a minute. Quinn replied.

Keeping up with your dancing? Maisie asked.

I need another lesson. You? How's it been since your grand win at the feis?

Wiped out for the first time in a while today. Ankle the size of a football.

Hugs.

Monday. Quinn posted.

???

My mother's client bailed. She says I can have the van and our driver for the first Monday of the half-term holidays. She can take us to Inis Mor.

I'm in!!! Maisie replied. She looked at her swollen ankle. Never could she have imagined she'd be glad to be injured. But the bum ankle meant she couldn't dance for several days, so she could slip off to the Aran Islands without guilt. No one on the dance squad could fault her for wanting to ease her way back into the studio. She'd need a Monday off for the next few weeks, and the trip west would be the perfect holiday from pressure. As long as her mother agreed.

100% responded Ravi.

Friend trip! They all smiled when they saw Tadgh's response. Even Quinn gave it a like.

Freya?

It was Ravi who asked. Freya wanted to go. Badly. But she was afraid her mother would want to milk every last minute of her time.

Have to see.

Make it happen. Quinn had no understanding of her life, Freya sighed to herself.

Will try.

And with that, arrangements were made to meet at 8am on the first Monday of the half term holiday. Quinn thought it would be ironic to meet at the bus depot. The others agreed. After they signed off, Freya went in search of her mother.

To her surprise, her mother was sitting in the lounge with the twins, smoking a stubby cigarette as she watched them wrestle. She didn't seem to mind at all when they knocked into the end table and sent the remote for the telly flying across the wooden floor. Freya sat on the edge of the couch.

"I want to go to St. Dymphna's for the day."

Her mother blew out a smoke ring. It hung in the air for a moment, suspended in the shaft of sunlight coming in through the back window, before disappearing.

"Why?"

"The misfits are gathering. The first Monday of the school holidays." Freya held her breath. If she made it sound like the trip was official, inferred it was part of The Misfits Club, she was certain she stood a better chance. "In Inis Mor."

"On the Aran Islands? On a random Monday? You're serious?"

"Yep."

"I've no money for bus fare."

Freya nodded. "I know. Quinn's mother ... his family will give us a ride. Please Mam, it's just for one day."

Her mother frowned. "I should say no."

Normally Freya would make a sarcastic remark. Tell her mother off. But since she'd returned from St. Dymphna's she'd had far less desire to speak her mind. Probably because she was speaking it on the webisodes and podcasts she'd been part of. Finally, Freya was heard.

"I suppose, since you did do everything asked of you at the camp and you're going on to that fancy private school that will be takin' the twins someday...."

Freya flinched. Nothing was ever just about her. But it was okay. She could play a bit part in her own life at home, since she had center stage in the real world.

Her mother slapped the side of her armchair. "Yes. You've done well for yourself, Freya. I primed you for success and finally you stepped up."

Freya clenched her fists to keep her cool. "Thank you."

As she turned to leave the room, her mother said, "Where do you think you're going? The twins need their dinner."

TWENTY-THREE

Freya fell into the deepest sleep she'd had in months. Before she went to bed she'd pulled out her calendar and marked off the number of days until the trip to Inis Mor. Then she tugged the books Lexie sent, all part of the reading list for her new school, counted up the number of pages she'd need to read each day to be done before Christmas Eve and entered all of her findings on the new diary Lexie had sent as a gift. She was in a deep sleep when her mobile buzzed. Disoriented, she turned over on her side. Two hours later, she woke and checked her messages. Two missed calls from Lexie. No text. That could not be good.

All of a sudden she was wide awake with worry. It was hours past midnight, far too late to call Lexie. She was tempted to text, but what if Lexie was the type who kept her mobile on at night? She'd probably be angry at being disturbed on a work night. So Freya stared at the ceiling, willing the hours to pass quickly. Finally, she dragged one of the books from her to be read pile out to the sitting room, cleared off the sofa and tried to read. But the words mashed together on the page. Something was wrong, she knew it.

She took a quick bath at sunrise before sitting down at the table to wait. She wanted to reach Lexie before the school day started. The nuns forbade mobiles in the classrooms. They weren't kidding when they said they had eyes in the back of their heads. Freya could not afford a demerit. She'd have to wait until the end of the day to connect with Lexie.

By the time she pulled her phone out she'd had two more missed calls from Lexie. Her chest was tight as she pressed call back.

"Ah, Freya. I was calling about your scholarship."

Freya looked up at her shabby school buildings. She'd been so excited to leave this place behind.

"Is something wrong?"

"You remember we discussed you wouldn't mention the others on your interviews."

"But...."

"I heard you on RTE."

"It was the right thing to do."

"Yes. You have a lot of integrity, Freya. I have to say, you gave me quite a scare." Lexie laughed.

Freya was puzzled. "Scare?"

"The admissions committee had admired the way you created The Misfits Club. Carved out a space for kids. Took ownership."

"And then I admitted I lied."

"Let's not call it a lie, rather a sin of omission."

Freya was afraid her knees were going to buckle. She was going to lose her scholarship because of the false claim about The Misfits Club. She leaned against the stone wall. The jagged stones dug into her flesh. She was sad, but not sorry. She'd done the right thing.

"Ironically it's worked in your favor."

"What?"

"Oh yes, the board of admissions said that the greatest demonstration of leadership is taking responsibility for poor judgments. Which you did. I just wanted you to know all is well. I was a bit concerned you'd be worrying that you'd somehow compromised your scholarship."

"That is a big relief."

"How's the term going otherwise? And what happened after the broadcast? Did you hear from the others?"

Everyone was excited for the trip to Inis Mor. Tadgh's mother insisted on finding out everyone's favorite color so she could send along five scarves as she'd heard it could be windy that time of year. Ravi offered to handle the food. He double checked that he had everyone's Turkish delight flavors, including Quinn's driver Agnes, who was partial to lemon. His father stayed up all night, cooking curries, baking naan and steaming rice so they'd be fresh for the journey. Maisie and Quinn compiled an epic playlist for the road trip. Freya brought bin bags, stuffed in her pockets, so they could clean up any litter along the way.

The morning of the trip, Freya was once more up before dawn. She loved this hour of the day, so ripe with possibilities, the sky a riot of changing hues. The city was still half asleep as she made her way along the quiet streets, past the pub owners setting out their chalkboards, the night shift workers staggering home and the occasional insomniac huddling in a doorway. She was pleased Quinn had chosen the bus depot for their point of departure. It was symmetrical, ending the journey where it all began. Freya loved predictability. It was why she adored maths. It was also why she'd been so horrid these past few months. She wasn't good with the unexpected, and the windfall of attention had turned her into a monster. She was still nervous about whether The Misfits had truly forgiven her when Maisie came toward her on the sidewalk outside the bus depot, arms open.

"Come here you dancing queen!" Maisie wrapped her in an enormous hug. "I've missed you."

Freya squeezed Maisie. "Same."

"Look at my moon boot." Maisie nodded down at her foot. "Next thing you know they'll be calling me big foot."

Freya laughed. "Ah, maybe we'll find him in the wormhole, down there with all the others."

They wandered toward the departures hall. Tadgh was already inside, once more with a large clutch of family. He looked just like his father. His mother was gently holding his arm. When she saw him smile at Freya and Maisie she whispered something in his left ear. He nodded, then brushed her off and came over to join them, carrying the sack of scarves. Freya smiled at his mother, who waved. Much to Tadgh's delight, after a final glance over their shoulders, his parents walked away.

A moment later Freya saw the long chauffeured car Quinn had arrived in glide up to the curb. A driver in a uniform hopped out of the car and opened Quinn's door. Freya was positive it was the same woman who'd dropped him off at the departures spot in the summer. Quinn stepped out of the car and said something to the driver. They both laughed.

"Quinn!" Tadgh called out, although Freya doubted he'd heard.

He was staring straight at Maisie as he walked toward the trio. Their eyes were locked. They smiled at each other, touching hands before Quinn hugged Freya and Tadgh, who could not stop smiling.

"Come on you lot, time for us to get in the car."

Freya panicked. She looked up at the big clock on the wall. It was well past eight. Where was Ravi? Had he decided not to come? She looked around. There was no sign of him. No one else seemed alarmed. They walked out to the curb. Freya tried to tamp down her disappoint as Quinn's driver introduced herself. Freya was so distraught she didn't hear the woman's name.

"I've never been in a chauffeured car before," Maisie whispered.

"Me neither," Freya said. "But I could get used to it."

Maisie laughed.

It was clear Tadgh was used to the sweet life. He asked the driver a number of questions about the make and model of the car, mentioning that his family had a similar model, only theirs was deep blue, not black. He patted the leather seats approvingly as he slid into place. Freya wanted to wait on the sidewalk for as long as possible. If she got into the car, she was convinced it meant Ravi would not be coming. However, she had no choice when Maisie nudged her to get into the car. Reluctantly she climbed inside, taking a place in the middle. Maisie sat across from her. Quinn remained on the sidewalk.

Freya heard Ravi before she saw him.

"Sorry I'm late, the first two batches of naan were a bit burnt so my father insisted on making new ones."

"Worth the wait, and thanks a mil," Quinn said.

He and the driver took Ravi's bags and locked them away in the boot.

"Wait!"

Freya heard the boot open again.

"Can't forget the sweets for the road."

"Good man," Quinn said.

Ravi climbed into the car and over Maisie. He wiggled his way along the seat, until he was next to Freya.

"Hi."

He smiled.

She smiled in return.

Quinn got into the car and sat next to Maisie. A moment later, the driver took her place. The engine roared to life and she pulled out into the mounting traffic.

Freya looked around at her friends. "I'm just so sorry."

"Apologies have already been accepted," Quinn said.

Freya shook her head. "Apologies yes, but you're due an explanation. Honestly my head was so swollen it wouldn't have fit into the car a few months ago. I let everything get to me. I wanted to be seen. Everywhere. So my da would be proud of me. Be sorry he left and come home."

"And?" Maisie asked.

"I never heard from him."

"That's unfair," Ravi said. "He shouldn't have done that to you. Totally his loss. You're so cool."

"Cool," Tadgh echoed.

Freya smiled. "Thanks."

The car came to a stop at a red light. Three girls were standing on the street corner, picking up all the trash gathered on the pavement. Next to them was a big sign that read, "Misfits Make the World a Better Place."

"We did that," Quinn said. "Epic."

"Legend," Ravi added.

"It is amazing," Maisie said. "Lots of girls at the feis are talking about cleaning up in the new places we visit. Some of the squads are carrying bin bags when they travel. It's incredible."

They watched as the city disappeared, replaced by the smaller towns that ringed the capitol and then finally the little villages of the countryside. Freya vowed to herself that one day she'd stop at every pub along the way.

"Time for a snack." Ravi opened the bag he'd dragged into the car. Inside was a cornucopia of sweets. Turkish delight, candy bars and little bags of gummies.

"I've your favorite, Freya. Lime gummies."

"Thanks."

"I'm still sad," Tadgh said as they approached Galway. "I wanted Aine to make an elixir. Bring the animals back to life."

"They're not dead, Tadgh. They're not even gone," Maisie said gently.

"Still. Sad."

"They're not forgotten, Tadgh. People keep coming into The Right Rice now, asking to see my animal drawings. Every time someone studies one of the sketches, I tell them to look up the animals. Take action so no more will go extinct."

"That's really smart," Freya said.

"Just doing my part," Ravi replied.

They sped through Galway, past all the shops and pubs and on toward the ferry. The port was virtually empty.

"No tourists this time of year," Quinn's driver called out from the front. "You lot are going to have a private cruise to Inis Mor."

She pulled the car into the lot near the dock. There were only two others waiting to cross.

The sea was rough and the sharp wind stung their cheeks. It was perfect. They stood at the edge of the craft, watching the clouds spin across the horizon as the waves tossed the ferry. When it landed they smiled at each other.

"Horrible thought," Maisie said. "Anyone have any idea how to get to St. Dymphna's?"

Freya was surprised. Surely Maisie had her phone? She looked at her friend. Maisie winked. Freya smiled. She understood. Maisie wanted to replay the summer. They all did.

"We all rely on Quinn," Tadgh said. "The human GPS."

Quinn laughed. "Something like that. Sure I know the way." He pointed to a spot in the distance. "Don't you recognize that rock formation?"

"All this limestone has always looked kind of the same to me," Maisie confessed.

"Why should we go to St. Dymphna's?" Tadgh asked.

"Fair point. I just thought maybe we'd want to see the place again, now that we're officially inmates."

"Inmates who broke out," Tadgh said. "They can't hold us there anymore."

Everyone laughed.

"I'd like to see it," Ravi said. "We've the time. It's a small island."

They walked along the uneven roads, past the low slung white washed farmhouses, the sheep grazing on the long grasses, and the wild horses galloping past the wildflowers. As they crested the small hill leading to the school, Ravi looked over at Freya, then dropped back a bit behind the others. Freya joined him.

"I saw you several times. Outside The Right Rice. Why didn't you come in?"

Freya heard the hurt in his voice. "I thought you wouldn't want to see me."

"I'd never not want to see you." Ravi stretched out his hand.

Freya slipped his fingers between his. They were warm and fitted her hand perfectly. They looked at each other and smiled.

Maisie looked back over her shoulder and smiled. "'bout time," she mouthed.

St. Dymphna's Holiday Academy loomed ahead. They all remembered that first day, hiking up the hill to the fenced structures, exhaustion mingled with fear. The hill was as steep as they remembered and the fence firmly in place. Only now, without the camp counselors in green shirts and the threat of the unknown, it didn't seem so foreboding.

"It looks almost ordinary," Freya said.

"Yeah, not sure why we were always huddled in our bunks," Maisie said.

The holiday academy was closed for the season. Like the rest of the island it was desolate. Almost forlorn. The stone statue of St. Dymphna was covered in mold and in desperate need of a good scrub.

"What do you think the counselors do in the off season?" Ravi asked.

"They run Mountjoy Prison," Quinn said.

Everyone laughed.

Freya exhaled. There was no need to tell them just yet what she knew about Lexie, Brie and Seamus.

"Any desire to mount the fence?" Quinn asked.

They looked at each other.

"No!"

"What if we get stuck in there?" Tadgh's voice shook.

"Fair play, we've seen the joint. Let's go visit Aine."

"Can't wait to see her again," Maisie said.

"I can't wait to see the bees."

"She's going to die when she hears about The Misfits Club going viral," Ravi said. He smiled at Freya. Although they were no longer holding hands, they still felt a connection running between them. "I know she'll be pleased you were out there for the animals."

"I hope so," Freya said. "She's the coolest woman I have ever met."

"A true one-off," Quinn said.

It was quiet as they headed into the hollow. Aine's cottage was much more rundown than any of them remembered. It had the same air of abandonment about it that Freya recalled from their first visit. Perhaps, she thought with dismay, Aine was away.

Quinn raced to the space where the hives once stood.

"The bees are gone!" Quinn practically shouted. "There are no hives."

An additional two windows were also missing from the front room. One entire side of the house was completely open to the elements.

"Mind your heads!" Freya cried as two birds flew out of the space that had previously held the sun porch where they'd shared scones.

Maisie heard a bell. She jerked her head in the direction of the noise. An older man was walking his dog along the road, ringing a bell every time the dog ran too far ahead. She scampered up to the road.

"Hiya sir."

"Hello there." He looked past her, to Freya, Quinn, Ravi and Tadgh. "No trouble, okay? We don't take kindly to smoking or drinking in the ruins in these parts."

"Ruins?" Maisie shook her head. "No, this is the home of our friend, Aine. From Limerick."

The man stroked his rough beard. "Aine? From Limerick?" He shook his head. "You've got it all wrong. There's no such person in all of Inis Moor. And that house, if you can even call it that at this point, has been in ruins for hundreds of years. No one's lived there in ages. You lot had best be careful. Don't go prowling around in that place, it could cave in on you."

His dog raced ahead. He rang the bell as he chased after her.

"We heard," Quinn said when Maisie rejoined them.

"What's going on?"

They walked through the space where a long, floor to

ceiling window once stood. The kitchen was gone. No more copper pots, no herbs, no fireplace. Just rundown remains. Farther on, the old computer room was also a void. There were no maps on the walls and certainly no modems, desktops or printers.

"I don't understand." Freya frowned.

"It's okay. Sometimes we're not meant to understand," Tadgh said.

"Well I hope wherever she is, she's all right," Maisie said.

"Don't worry about Aine," Ravi said. "She's the type who can always look after herself."

"Enough of this, who wants to visit the wormhole?" Quinn asked.

They all raised their hands.

They no longer needed Quinn to lead the way. They'd traveled the path to the serpent's lair enough times they could each find it on their own if needed.

There was no one on the road and no one at the wormhole. They smiled at each other as they approached the sunken limestone formation. The jade, gray and deep blue waters swirled, splashing frothy waves onto the rocks.

"I forgot how slippery it is," Maisie said, looking down at the boot on her foot.

"I got you." Quinn stretched out his hand.

Freya and Ravi also held hands. Not wanting Tadgh to feel left out, the way she did when her twin sisters babbled to each other in a language only they could understand, Freya grabbed Tadgh's hand as well. They gingerly made their way along the slick rocks, down to the lower level, and sat near the entrance to the wormhole.

"What's the story with the tides, Quinn?" Ravi shouted over the wind. "How long do we have down here before these rocks are under the water?"

"We've an hour max," Quinn said. "Unless you want to go back into the serpent's lair."

"No," Freya said. "Too risky."

"I agree."

"So do I."

"Best left to memory."

"Fine, I'm outnumbered."

They sat on the rocks and watched the water disappear into the wormhole. They were all hopeful that somehow one of the animals would pop up and greet them, but they saw nothing. Not even seals.

"I don't understand what happened. We all know what we saw, right?" Maisie asked.

They all shook their head.

"And yet here we are. How do you explain...."

"You can't," Quinn said.

"Maybe it doesn't matter."

They all turned to Tadgh.

"What do you mean?" Maisie asked.

"Maybe the only thing that's important is how we interpret what happens to us in life."

"I agree with that," Freya said. "Events are neutral but for the meaning we assign them."

Maisie wasn't convinced. "But I know what I saw. I know what we all saw."

Quinn put his arm around her shoulder.

"Thoughts, Tadgh?" Quinn asked.

"Maybe we were meant to come here because we were the endangered animals. The five of us, all very close to extinction. Maybe what we really saved was ourselves."

The water in the wormhole went still and then parted. For an instant they glimpsed the other world. The bears were dancing. The grey wolves were running, ears back, tails high.

Beyond them the whales frolicked in the water as sun streamed onto a garden of exotic flowers. An enormous wave crashed and the vision was gone.

Freya looked out to sea, beyond the serpent's lair, then back at her beloved friends.

"Long live the misfits!"

THE END

ABOUT THE AUTHOR

Therese Gilardi's poetry, essays and short fiction have appeared in numerous journals and anthologies including "Literary Mama," "Mom Egg Review," "Onthebus," "Punchnel's," "Ariel Chart" and "The Diary, The Detective and The Dublin Irish Festival."

Therese is the author of the novels "Narvla's Celtic New Year," "The Last Romance," "Matching Wits with Venus," "Isabelle the Imaginist" and the poetry collection "The Arsenic of Archangels."

facebook.com/theresegilardiauthor

Made in USA - North Chelmsford, MA
1377129_9780986281198
07.18.2023 1639